IN THE
SHADOWS

A STORY ABOUT STANDING STRONG TOGETHER

IN THE SHADOWS

CAROL PATRICIA RICHARDSON

proving
press

Book Design & Production:
Columbus Publishing Lab
www.ColumbusPublishingLab.com

Paperback ISBN: 978-1-63337-428-7
E-Book ISBN: 978-1-63337-429-4

Printed in the United States of America
13 5 7 9 10 8 6 4 2

Front cover character paintings by
Ophelia Hernandez Hiestand

DEDICATION

T his book is dedicated to the two Cs, my forever friends, and to an amazing group of homeschool students whose honesty profoundly informed and shaped the final version of the book. They are Robert D. Cook, Isabelle Cook, Finnean Malley, Caroline R. Mocharski, Joseph Tayal, Miri Washer, Noelle Wirebaugh, and Ali Malley, their teacher.

In the Shadows is also dedicated to the memory of the countless men, women, and children who have lost their lives on the migrant trail, and to the families who mourn for them, and for the communities that suffer the divisions that borders wreak on us all.

(resource: https://azmigranttrail.com)

AUTHOR'S NOTE

In the Shadows is a work of fiction, but it is based on historical events. In the spring of 1954, President Dwight D. Eisenhower (Ike) launched Operation Wetback, an initiative to remove thousands of undocumented workers from the United States. Most of those targeted were migrants from Mexico. In what is often described as a quasi-military operation, U.S. Border Patrol agents, along with state and local law enforcement officers, methodically rounded up Mexican and Mexican-American workers. With guns in hand, the agents and officers showed up in agricultural fields in Texas and California, and in bus and train stations, restaurants, hotels, and meat-packing plants in Chicago and other communities across the country—wherever Mexican migrants worked. The result was widespread fear and abuse.

On the first day alone of Operation Wetback, as many

as 4,800 people were apprehended in military-style sweeps. By the end of the year, the Immigration and Naturalization Service (INS) claimed 1,100,000 were deported—some on their own out of fear. There were reports of beatings, intimidation, and blatant disregard for civil liberty rights. Hundreds of families were torn apart. Many who were deported were American citizens of Mexican heritage.

Operation Wetback occurred nearly seventy years ago, and I fear that we have learned little from our past mistakes. *In the Shadows* is an effort to put a human face on inhuman immigration policies that have plagued our country before and since, even to the present day.

—C. Richardson

PROLOGUE

I turned twelve in May of 1954, just after school ended and summer vacation began. Mom made red velvet cake with cream cheese icing, and Daddy brought home a gallon of Blue Bell's best vanilla ice cream. My two favorite girlfriends came to celebrate my birthday, and Daddy made us laugh all through supper with one lame joke after another. Jimmy, the neighbor kid, crashed the party just in time for dessert.

That's how the summer started its meandering way toward September when school would claim us again. And if it had ended like it started, that summer would have become just another sweet dessert, melted into my memory like the birthday ice cream.

But that's not what happened, and it's the "what happened" part that I want to tell you about.

CHAPTER 1

y name is Blue, but that's not the name on my birth certificate. When I was born, the doctor wrote down *Madeline Elizabeth Baxter* on the official paper because that's what Mom told him. That name came from a kid's book Mom liked, and it's why she chose it. But Madeline didn't fit me. Fortunately, my GramZees knew that right away.

I read the book *Madeline* when I was seven. It's a tale about twelve girls—one called Madeline, of course—who live at a boarding school in a fancy house in the middle of Paris, which, since it's the capital of France, is an important and fast-moving place. My life is not at all like that—not even close. I go to a come-home-at-night school and live in a barn-shaped house in a tiny Ohio town called Shortstop, which is not the capital of anything. Freight trains run through our little burg, so maybe that counts for something.

A five-train day is about as busy as it gets in Shortstop, except when the horse races come to town. But I'll get to that later.

Book-Madeline and her boarding school friends go everywhere "in two straight lines." Headed to the park? Straight lines. To the zoo? Lock-step formation to get there. Even at age seven, I thought the straight-line stuff was plenty weird. How can a girl have any fun if she always walks the line? Book Madeline is a straight-line kind of girl. I am not.

And neither is my grandmother. GramZees took over all the new-baby care when Mom came home from the hospital, and right away she knew my name was all wrong. I guess she had read about straight-line Madeline, and she was having none of it for me. Without asking anyone's permission, she ditched Madeline and started calling me Blue.

My new namesake was a raucous blue jay that squawked right outside the nursery window and got everyone's attention. The boisterous jaybird delighted GramZees. "I named you Blue," she tells me now, "so's you'll be free like a bird and raise a ruckus if need be." I still don't really understand what that means, but GramZees says I'll know when the time comes.

GramZees has wispy white hair that fuzzes and frizzes all over her head like cotton candy gone wild. And she is wiry thin—frail-looking, some would say. People could underestimate her, but that would be a big mistake. My grandma is a formidable woman, and she has decided ideas

2

on a bunch of topics. She stands up for her opinions and stands by her "causes." Daddy calls her a do-gooder. I call her GramZees the Great.

I got the GramZees idea from a *Classic Comics* story. The top pharaoh in ancient Egypt was called Ramses the Great. Ramses. GramZees. Get it? Ramses got "the Great" added to his name because of all the good things he did for people. And that's the same reason I gave GramZees her nickname.

Every summer, my grandma comes from California to stay with us in Ohio, but this year she's arriving later than usual. One of her causes kept her home. "I just can't leave those families in such a fix," she reported when she wrote to say her trip east was delayed. Her details were skimpy, but it had to do with Mexican workers who pick vegetables near where she lives. I'm sure we will get the full story about the "fix" the families are in when GramZees arrives on the cross-country train today.

Mom and I want to cook a special welcome-back supper, so we are making plans over breakfast. "Mommy craves her cornbread," says Mom, thinking out loud, "and anything we can get out of the garden. Maybe I'll fix some fresh lettuce with hot bacon dressing. What do you think about fried chicken, too?" Mom asks me, but mostly herself. "And applesauce cake for sure," she finishes. "You can make the cake, Blue." She turns to me, her menu settled. Okay by me. Chicken and cake, what's not to like?

Around six, Mom tells me to set the table. She's busy over the stove frying up a batch of cut-up spring chicken that she's battered with buttermilk and coated in flour. The tantalizing aroma drifts through the house and makes my mouth water. Mom has on her best house dress with pink flowers, which she keeps protected by a full apron while she cooks. I've chosen a bright blue button-up shirt for myself and pedal pusher pants that come to my knees. GramZees sent me the shirt for Christmas, and I want her to see how good it looks.

When I have all the plates and silverware in place, the ice tea glasses just to the right of each knife, and the striped napkins on the left by each fork, I stop futzing over the table and decide to check my applesauce cake for maybe the tenth time. I want to be sure the icing has stayed put and not run down the sides to circle the cake like a moat. The cake is perfect, just as it was the last time I looked. All is well.

The chicken's in the oven to stay warm, and the table is beautiful with a bowl of fresh flowers in the middle. There's nothing left undone, but still Mom and I putter around nervously in the kitchen. "Hope your daddy didn't get stopped by a freight train," Mom frets. "Those engineers take their sweet time clearing the track — think nobody's got anything to do but them." I nod my head to agree, and at the same time lift the cake cover to take one more look.

Just when we can't stand another minute's wait, the gravel finally crunches in the driveway outside the kitchen window. Daddy eases our '48 Chevy to a stop by the side of the house, and Mom and I are out the back door before GramZees's feet touch the ground.

"Lordy, Lordy," my grandma blusters, "you two are a beautiful sight!" She throws her arms open to us, and I melt into her embrace. GramZees is finally here. Now summer can really get going.

CHAPTER 2

"Where've you been?" Mom asks when I walk into the kitchen. She and GramZees stand side-by-side at the counter to cook and chat together like they do almost every night. GramZees has been here a week, and we have settled into the rhythm of summer. Mom's question takes me by surprise, and I don't answer. I've been up on the train tracks most of the day, but I don't want to say. Mom believes I should have better things to do than walk the railroad.

GramZees glances up. She has noticed my hesitation, but fortunately, Mom seems not to. She is distracted by a head of green cabbage she's shaving into fine slivers. "Get your apron on, Blue," Mom directs without looking up, "and mix up some slaw dressing." My late arrival doesn't matter anymore because there is supper to finish. GramZees winks at me. She knows I've escaped the "talk."

I scrounge in the icebox for mayonnaise to start the dressing. Our cat hears the icebox door and wanders in from his window perch in the front room. He rubs once against my leg as he passes, then he sits on his haunches to stare at me with his demanding yellow eyes. Roscoe wants milk, and he wants it now! I understand that this is his first ask. If I procrastinate, his second pass won't be so solicitous or gentle. Roscoe will bite me. It will be just a nip on my bare calf, but enough to notice and plenty to get his message across. I go back to the icebox for the buttermilk bottle. Buttermilk is the only milk Roscoe will drink. "Why do we put up with him?" Mom asks no one in particular. Roscoe saunters to his food bowl in full command of the situation.

"Your daddy needs help in the garden tonight," Mom says to me as she sets the bowl full of slaw in my direction to dress. "He wants to get the tomatoes planted. Your grandma and I will do up supper dishes so you can get started early."

"Sure," I say, and smile. Being outside in the garden with Daddy is always better than dirty dishes.

Lightning bugs are the only light by the time Daddy and I get the last of the tomatoes into the ground. The project took much longer than expected, mostly because of the watering. The outside spigot pokes out on the kitchen side of the house, but it's a long way to the garden at the far end of our acre. Daddy rigged two hoses together, but even that falls short of the job. The black double-hose snakes only as far as the gooseberry bush, about mid-yard. I had to go back for bucket after bucket of water to fill all the holes where Daddy planted tomato starts.

It was a wet spring and Daddy couldn't get the garden plowed as early as he had hoped. But even so, the spring garden is a marvel. Long rows of beans and corn peek through the soil, and crinkly blue-green kale is ready for harvest. We've been eating lettuce and green onions for a while now, and Mom whipped up a bowl of buttery new peas a couple of days ago.

"Let's carry the tools to the garage," Daddy finally says when the last of the tomatoes are set. I slide the bucket handle up my arm and gather the hoe and shovel. Daddy wheels the hand plow toward the house. His is a two-handed job.

"'Night, girls," we say softly to Bess and Barkey, Daddy's rabbit dogs. The beagles are already hunkered down for the night. Daddy built them a roomy pen with wooden doghouses the first week we moved from the country into town. "Bess and Barkey need a new home too," Daddy had reasoned out loud when Mom raised an eyebrow at the bill for the fence wire and the lumber. The beagles are Daddy's prize trackers, and he takes good care of them—more than good, Mom would argue.

Daddy and I thread our way in the dark, past the dog pen and the apple tree that shades it. The tree also shades the garden shed. We used to store our tools there, but now it's empty. "Roof's leaking," Daddy reported when he went looking for lime to spread on the garden. The twenty-five-pound bag of powder had turned hard from water that dripped through the shed roof during the winter. Same with bags of fertilizer and bean-bug dust, and the metal-ended garden tools were spotted with rust. We had to clean out the shed and move everything to shelves in the garage. Daddy says he'll fix the roof when he has time, but it hasn't happened yet. Maybe not till fall.

We slip into the dark garage through the side door, and I lean the hoe and shovel against the cinder block wall. Daddy flips the plow to rest upside down on its wide-spread wooden handles. "You can pull the hose to the side of the house in the morning," Daddy says. "We've done enough for now."

As we shuffle the final steps toward the house, the night stillness settles over everything. GramZees always says it's like a deep sigh is exhaling the day. Only the kitchen light shows through the screen to guide the way inside.

Summer's relaxed, but besides the garden, I still have lots of jobs. I mow our grass on Wednesdays and cut Mrs. Sniff's yard on Thursdays, and maybe into Friday if she wants the back half-acre cut too, which is every couple of weeks or so. Mrs. Sniff's back lot is a hard mow because the sawgrass grows up thick and tall, well above my ankles, and the razor-sharp grass blades slice into my legs. I wish she'd either let me cut the back every week, so it won't get a head start on me, or just let it grow up tall like it wants to. But she pays me a dollar for the easy weeks and two when I get the back lot too, so I don't complain. Some weeks I also cut Mrs. Gallon's grass next door, but only if Mr. Gallon is ailing or just doesn't want to bother. Occasionally I'll mow Mr. Turney's on the other side of us if he's too busy running his pool hall in town and can't get to it himself.

I have my eye on a new Huffy bike for sale at Miller's Hardware up on Main Street, and I'm savin' up $54.99 to buy it before school starts. I keep my loot in a cigar box and count it out a couple times a week to see how I'm doing. I have $17 so far, still a long way to go. The bike is a beauty — the Deluxe model Classic Cruiser with a "hand-painted" tank and chain guard and a woven basket in front. The bike is blue, of course.

Besides payin' work, I've got family jobs too. But they don't pay anything. When I complained about the freebies, Mom raised an eyebrow and asked, "You wanna start paying rent instead?" But I persisted, so she added, "Do you eat here?" I stopped grumbling a couple of summers back and accepted that my "family" jobs are gratis. I hoe corn when Daddy says to, weed between the rows of beans to keep the thistles out, and squash fat tomato worms that gorge themselves green on tomato leaves. Tomato worms will strip a plant clean if you let 'em go.

I also pick stuff from the garden for Mom—usually green beans or lettuce, but sometimes rhubarb and straw-berries from the patch at the edge of the garden. A straw-berry-rhubarb day is special, because it means Mom or GramZees is making a pie for dessert.

But even with all my jobs, summer days are still mostly mine to fill, and Jimmy Mick is part of the filling plan. The Micks live two doors up from our place, just on the other side of the Gallons' house. Jimmy is my age and a boy, of course. At school we pretend to barely know each other and certainly do not own up to being friends. But summertime on Norwood Street is a different thing.

"Wanna do the track today?" Jimmy asks. We are in the front-porch swing watching bees hover over the honeysuckle vine. Roscoe is watching the bees too, and he takes a half-hearted swing at any that buzz within range. It's a hot lazy day and we need something to do. The railroad tracks run behind our houses on the far end of our back lots, and they are an essential part of our summer entertainment.

"Sure," I say, eagerly piling on the idea. "Got any pennies?" I dig into my pocket while I ask Jimmy. He fishes a copper coin from his jeans at the same time I find one in mine. Pennies in hand, we leave the bees to their flowers and amble through the backyard into the garden. We pick a handful of the last strawberries on the way by the patch and agree that the first berries and the last berries are always the sweetest of the season. We reach the ridge where the sweet potatoes twirl their shiny leaves along the back edge of the garden, and from there, we scramble up the weedy hill onto the chunky gravel in the railroad bed.

The railroad's been running by this very spot for more than a hundred years. That's what Mr. Winter told Jimmy and me. Mr. Winter's lived in Shortstop forever and he's really old, so maybe he knows. He says the railroad was here even before there was a town. When the first tracks were laid, there weren't any houses or stores or even many people. But the steam engines made short, quick stops here to take on water from the towers the railroad company built. That's how Shortstop got its name. Or so Mr. Winter said. I think the story's probably true because the water fill-up towers are still here. And they still work. Jimmy and I have watched lots of steam locomotives take on water in front of Winter's store. That's where the towers are: two of them, one for trains coming from the north and one for those from the south.

Jimmy and I can spend hours speculating about where the trains we see started out. When I asked Daddy, he guessed maybe Kentucky or Georgia or as far south as Texas even. But, he said, east-west tracks crisscross the rails coming up from the south and join the tracks going north. "So, there's no tellin' where the trains came from originally," was his final conclusion.

Passenger trains like the one GramZees rode on from California are a rare occasion. If one does happen by, Jimmy and I flap our arms and go wild to get the passengers' attention. If they notice and wave back, we consider it a really good day at the track.

Freight trains are the usual fare. Long trails of loaded boxcars and tankers filled with chemicals roll through several times a day. They teeter back and forth like they might topple at any time, and some years back, they did. There was a train wreck on the track right behind our house, which wasn't our house yet. A whole line of boxcars twisted themselves up and fell over into the garden. Sometimes we still find bullets that got left behind in the cleanup. Daddy said the wrecked train was carrying ammunition for the war.

Lately Jimmy and I see more and more flatbed cars coming by stacked with giant semi-truck trailers. We speculate on the trailers' contents. "A lot of 'em are loaded with stuff made overseas," Jimmy reports, information he learned from his Aunt Liddie. And she might be right. Now that World War II is over, cheap not-made-in-America junk is filling up the stores, Daddy says, and he's hopping mad about it because if it's not made here, it takes our workers' jobs. But there's no stopping it, Mom says. I even saw some of the cheap stuff for sale here in Shortstop at the Red in White store. It probably got hauled here on a train that passed right behind our house.

And maybe that's true for the hamburger meat Mr. Handman sells at the IGA grocery up on Main Street. The same three-pounds-for-a-dollar ground chuck that we buy for sloppy joes might have rolled by our house. Of course, the hamburger on the train still had four legs. I see the cattle cars almost every day. The poor frightened creatures bawl all the way from Chicago where there's a huge stockyard, and some of them get off in Ohio to meet their bad end in the slaughterhouse out on Rings Road. Or so Jimmy and I surmise.

We spend hours concocting train stories. But that's just one of the summertime diversions the railroad tracks offer. Some afternoons, Jimmy and I climb onto the railroad bed just to walk and see what we see. When we decide it's a walk-the-track day, the big decision is whether to head south or north. The southern route cuts through the fields and pastures outside of town. About a mile out, there's a gnarly apple orchard just a few steps from the track. The trees are past prime, but they still produce a few yellow apples in the spring and some Winesaps in the fall. Jimmy and I like them both and fill our pockets when the season's right.

About a half mile beyond the orchard, we have a hideout. It's in a grove of scrubby maple saplings, and we take our apples there so we can eat and talk...and smoke. Jimmy brings Chesterfields when he can sneak them from his dad's pack, and I sometimes bring a couple of Raleighs from Mom's stash. Lately, though, I steer clear of the Raleighs because Mom gave me a look last time her cigarettes went missing. She may be on to me.

The northbound track passes through the main part of town and offers a different kind of fun—like Willie's Drug Store that's just a block from the main crossing. Willie's is a boring drug store in every way, but for two notable exceptions. One is the lunch counter/soda fountain in the rear where you can get a burger and fries special. Or you can skip the lunch menu and go straight for the ice cream, which is what Jimmy and I usually do. Mr. Willie is a marvel with sundaes. He drizzles two big scoops of vanilla with thick steam-rising-off-it hot fudge that he sprinkles with chopped walnuts and mounds with whipped cream that hisses from the can. He tops his creations with a stemmed cherry so red you know it comes from a jar instead of a tree. Mr. Willie's sundaes are well worth the fifty-cent cost, but usually we don't have that much. If we're on our budget plan, we opt for cones instead. A triple dipper is just fifteen cents.

But before we get to the ice cream at Willie's, we pass a wall lined with magazines. The magazine display is the store's second notable exception to boring. Willie's Drug has an impressive array of reading material. The display shelves run from the floor to the ceiling. The topmost racks hold the "girlies," which is what we call the magazines with slinky blond women and muscly men on the covers. The girlies are meant to be out of reach for anyone under six feet, but just in case, Mrs. Willie is there to keep watch. She stands at the cash register across the aisle and aims hostile stares to discourage underage peeking.

But no matter, we have plenty to keep us entertained. The entire bottom two rows are dedicated to comic books. The newest issues flash at us in full color: *Nancy and Sluggo*, *Wonder Woman*, *Archie*, and my favorite, *Classic Comics*. *Classic Comics* has exotic full-color drawings of the gods and goddesses from ancient Egypt, Greece, and Rome. I was totally captivated the first time I spotted them. And, of course, *Classic Comics* was the inspiration for the GramZees nickname. Jimmy and I can stand by the racks and read comics all afternoon if we want and never spend a dime.

But none of that is on our minds today. We are standing on the railroad track behind my house waiting for a train to pass. Jimmy and I drop to our knees and lean our ears to the gleaming rail. We don't talk. We just listen for the rumble of a locomotive to travel to us through the steel.

"What'd you think? Five minutes?" Jimmy raises his head and the question.

"'Bout that, I'd say." We carefully lay our pennies on the rail top. "I'm heads," I call, though we both know it won't matter in the end. The train wheels fling the pennies off the rail helter-skelter into the gravel regardless of which side is up at the start.

"Here she comes," Jimmy says as he steps off the thick wooden tie to the garden edge. "Coming from the south, so maybe a load of Kentucky coal," he says hopefully. Everybody knows that coal trains are best for flattening pennies. And especially when the cars are pulled by steam locomotives. Those trains are long, slow, and really heavy. Light-loaded diesels run faster and throw the pennies to the side too soon to get flattened properly.

Jimmy and I see the sky-high plumes of smoke billowing from the locomotive, but it's not pulling coal like we hoped. Instead, we watch as a long line of empty box-cars bang by. Some are yellow, others rusty-red, but most are black. Their big sliding doors are thrown open on both sides, and light shines through from one side to the other.

"You see that?" I yell over the train ruckus.

Jimmy looks at me.

"Hoboes." I point to two men sitting in the doorway of one dingy red car that's rumbling toward us. They are sitting on the boxcar floor with their legs hanging relaxed and loose over the edge to the outside. One man is bareheaded, and the other tips his hat in a salute to us. I raise my hand to wave as they roll by.

"Where do you think they're headed?" I wonder out loud as the caboose trails out of sight. Jimmy and I squat close to the ground in search of our flattened pennies in the crushed gravel.

"Who?" Jimmy is distracted.

"The hoboes. In the boxcar."

"Oh. Who knows?" Jimmy's not interested. But my curiosity twitters.

"Maybe Detroit," I say, picking it up again. "My dad says workers from down south are moving north for jobs in the auto plants. A lot of 'em are Negroes trying to find decent-paying jobs, Daddy says. They talk about it at his union meetings. Daddy thinks that's a good thing, 'cause everyone should have a chance to do better."

"Those hoboes on the train were white," Jimmy points out as he looks up, a little interested now. "Maybe they're just ridin' the rails. Some people do that, ya know — hop into boxcars and go wherever the train's headed." Both of us go silent for a minute as we consider what that might be like.

"Where do you suppose they get their food? They can't plant a garden." I am dismayed. A garden is essential if you want to eat good. At least to my way of thinking. "And where do they get cleaned up? Boxcars don't have bathtubs."

Jimmy smiles at that. Avoiding the bathtub appeals to him.

"And how can they keep a job and tend to their families if they're hopping on trains all the time?" I go on while

Jimmy still considers the no-bathtub advantage. "I just can't see how the hobo thing could work out." I shake my head.

"I don't know any more about it." Jimmy's done with bathtubs and hoboes. "But I do know about Mr. Flathead Lincoln." He holds up a piece of sliver-thin copper. The hobo train has transformed his penny into a shiny quarter-sized disc. Jimmy slides his prize into his jeans pocket.

I bring up my questions about hobo life again when I am hoeing weeds in the bean patch alongside Daddy after supper. "Do hoboes live in their boxcars all year long?"

Daddy pauses to lean on the hoe while he considers. "Would be really cold in the winter if they did." I can tell he's rolling the question in his mind, taking it seriously. Daddy doesn't treat me like a kid who just asks silly questions and never thinks about anything important. "I'd say they have to stay south in the winter," Daddy adds after a minute, "and hop the trains when they want to find work. Maybe go to Georgia to pick peaches in the summer and up to New York State to pick apples in October. Something like that. But that's just a guess." Daddy hoe-chops a tall thistle that's sprung up between the plants.

Roscoe unexpectedly bolts from the bean row we are working. We didn't see him under the leaves, and Daddy's hoe disturbed his nap and almost got his tail. Roscoe huffs away. "You better take that tail of yours and skedaddle,"

Daddy says through a chuckle, "or next time I might chop it off." Roscoe casts a disdainful glance backward and flattens his ears—his last word on the subject.

"Do women hop trains too? What about kids?" I ask.

"Don't really know." Daddy keeps hoeing. "I've never seen any women or kids in the boxcars. But hoboing is illegal, and train-hoppers mostly hide to keep from bein' arrested. So that makes it hard to say who's really riding."

CHAPTER 3

"I'm headin' to the bookmobile," I call through the screen to the backyard. Mom is hanging clothes on the line and GramZees is snipping purple lilacs for the vase on the kitchen table. Roscoe is stretched out on the cool concrete by the garage. He's fixed on a fat robin wrangling a worm from the flower bed. "I'll be back in an hour or so," I tell Mom. Roscoe's eyelids droop. *Why chase birds?* He yawns. *The humans fill my bowl.*

I take off out the front door and head past the catawba tree at the end of the driveway. If I walk fast, I can be at the corner of Main and Norwood before the bookmobile arrives. I want to be first in line.

Shortstop's too little to have its own library, so the whole town depends on the bookmobile. If Mr. Handman at the IGA wants to study up on new trends in the grocery business, he borrows a book from the bookmobile.

If waitress Marge needs a good mystery to read on slow days at the restaurant, she knows where to get it. If someone is curious about hoboes, then the bookmobile is the place to go.

In the summertime, the library-on-wheels parks in front of the Methodist church every other Monday from one o'clock to three. The queue is usually long and always slow-moving. Being first in line is big on my mind as I hustle past Jimmy's house and the rose gardens in the Williams's front yard. I hail Mrs. Gerhes who is hosing down her front porch, and I throw up a hand to Mr. Knox who has stationed his ancient rocking chair close to the sidewalk so he can snag passersby. Mr. Knox is full of grand stories and long tales about this and that, but I am on a mission and I don't want to stop today.

After Mr. Knox, I cross over Norwood in front of Doc Carr's office and zip by a couple of patients who shuffle toward the doc's door. I can see ahead that the bookmobile hasn't come yet, but some folks are already waiting under the elm tree in front of the church parsonage. The Methodist preacher is chatting with a couple of kids who stand in line. "You've worked up a lather, Blue," Reverend Adams greets me. "You must be looking for a special book."

I like the preacher, but I always feel shy around him. We Baxters aren't a church-going family, though if we were, I guess we would go to the Methodist church. My other grandma is big on church, Daddy says, and Methodist to her bones, according to Mom. So Methodist is kinda in our family genes. Still, we don't belong to the Methodist church or the Catholic one either, which is the only other option in town. "Nothing against it," Mom said when I asked. "I just leave it to others." GramZees does too. And Daddy.

The preacher is making his way toward me now. Rev. Adams is a lanky crow of a man with a hooked-beak nose and black hair that is never quite combed. His blue eyes pierce everyone they touch, but his smile makes it okay somehow. "The Methodist preacher's a straight talker," Daddy said over supper one night. Being a straight talker is high on Daddy's good-qualities list. "He says what he means and means what he says," is how Daddy summed up Rev. Adams.

I have no experience with the preacher's straight talk, but he "feels" trustworthy to me, which is a requirement for preachers, I think, since people tell them all kinds of private things when they need advice. But, like I said, we Baxters aren't church-goers, so I don't expect I will be telling Rev. Adams any secrets or asking for advice.

"I was going to stop by your house later today, Blue." Rev. Adams puts his blue-eyed beam on me. "But here you are at the bookmobile! I should have guessed you would be." His words land with a grin.

Stop by our house? I do a double take. I'm confused and my face surely shows it, but Rev. Adams goes on.

"We're starting a Methodist Youth Fellowship this summer and the first meeting is this Sunday night at six. It's called 'MYF.' Why don't you come?" My tongue ties a knot on the roof of my mouth. Rev. Adams is hard to say no to. He has a way of making you feel special and at the same time letting you know he has high expectations. "Think you can make it?" he says, pushing on through my hesitation.

"Well...uh...maybe...sure." He's put me on the spot, and I can't think up a good excuse. The preacher's invited me to church before—getting people to join up is part of his job—but he's never been so direct or specific.

"Okay. Good! We'll see you in the church basement. Sunday. Six o'clock." The straight talker has the answer he wants. He turns on his smile and walks toward the church door just as the lime green bookmobile lumbers to a stop at the curb.

I watch the preacher disappear inside the church building. I'm already working my brain to think up an excuse to get out of Sunday night. My family's not churchy, as I said.

CHAPTER 4

"**G**ramZees! Mom! Look!" I've run all the way home from the IGA with groceries in one hand and a printed flyer in the other. The preacher who straight-talked me into a Sunday night worry has flown from my head — Wednesday is the only thing on my mind. I burst through the back door holding up one of the notices that are plastered on every telephone pole in town. *HARNESS RACES WEDNESDAY!*

Mom leans over the hot ironing board in the kitchen. She has just finished laying down the sharp crease in Daddy's dark gray work pants. Two wicker baskets take up the table. One is piled with fluffy dry clothes fresh from the line, and the other has balled-up pieces of clean damp laundry. GramZees stands by the table with her water-filled bottle. She pulls a blouse from the dry fluffy pile and sprinkles it lightly, rolls it up and puts it in the basket of damp pieces. The dampened clothes iron up nice with no wrinkles.

"I know the races start tomorrow." This is Mom's matter-of-fact reply to my energy. She glances up briefly from a damp shirt collar she has spread out on the board. She tries to hide her grin, but she can't. Or GramZees either. The three of us love the races!

"We're goin' on the first night, right?" I confirm as I start to put the groceries away in the icebox. The harness races run for forty nights at the fairgrounds track just a short walk from our house.

"Of course," Mom says. "Girls' night out," she adds, with a twinkle toward GramZees.

GramZees, Mom, and I have our "girls' night" every summer on opening night of the racing season. We go early and stay late. It's our treat to ourselves, Mom says, for all the hard work we do. Daddy never joins us. He says it's because he has to get up so early, but GramZees believes he's just being nice. He doesn't want to horn in on our fun.

Every year, we three "girls" get to the fairgrounds early to look at the race lineup for the night. We pick up the "Green Sheet" at the entrance gate, and it tells us everything we need to know — stuff like the horses' names.

"Names can tell you a lot," Mom always says; she won't bet on a horse with an ugly name. She picks ones like "Flying Fantastic" or "See-You-Later-Tater." Once she won big on a horse called "Annie's Girl." She chose it because she has a sister named Annie.

The Green Sheet also has information about the drivers. In harness racing, the driver holds onto long reins and sits spread-legged in a two-wheeled sulky cart the horse pulls around the dirt track. Bettors try to figure out which horse/driver team is best. Mom and GramZees say they study the names and the win/loss statistics in order to make their betting picks, but in the end, they seem to rely mostly on their gut to tell them which horse to put their money on. "You can kinda 'feel' the winner," GramZees believes, and Mom doesn't disagree.

"Our next-door neighbor's getting rich on the races," Daddy reports on Wednesday evening before we three take off for our night out. "Mr. Turney tells me he's gonna keep his pool hall open all night every night this summer while the horses are running. Says he'll haul in the dough."

"What about Sparkey's?" Mom wants to know about the beer joint next to the pool hall.

"Oh, you can bet they'll be open too," Daddy says. "Sparkey won't miss the chance to fill his cash register. None of 'em will. The money will come raining down on the merchants of Shortstop for forty days and forty nights." Daddy throws his hands to the sky like a TV preacher.

"It's biblical!" GramZees picks up. "Like Noah's flood." We all laugh. Then Daddy pushes his chair from the table and leaves to watch the evening news. Mom, GramZees, and I get up in a flurry to clear the dishes. We are done in a flash.

"Ready to go?" Mom asks as she wipes the sink dry.

"You bet!" GramZees grabs her purse from upstairs, and we go for the door. Mom is already on the porch. A long line of cars edges forward beside us as we walk along Norwood Street toward the fairgrounds. Hundreds of people—maybe thousands on a good night—come from all over to take their chances on the horses. Last year, GramZees was thrilled when she spotted a license plate from California.

Normally Shortstop is a slow, sleepy place where we know everyone and pretty much everything about them. People in town never lock their doors. There's no need. Strangers do not walk our streets. But when the races hit town, all that changes.

With the races come the stable hands and trainers, judges and officials—all the folks it takes to keep the horses running and people placing their bets. The well-paid workers rent sleeping space from local folks, bedding down in upstairs bedrooms or screened-in porches with sleeper-couches. Some of the workers come in pickup trucks that tow squat little trailer-houses behind them. They park in the grove of oak trees behind the barns at the fairgrounds; almost overnight, a trailer park takes root and sprouts inside the Shortstop town limits.

And there are the "boys"—though most seem like broken-down old men to me—who follow the races from town to town like hoboes. They hire on to muck the stalls and walk the lathered-up horses in endless cool-down circles after the workouts. These men are poor, Daddy says. They don't have money to rent a room in town, and they don't have trailer-houses to park in the oak grove. At night they bed down in the stalls next to the animals they tend during the day.

All these outsiders are a boom for Shortstop businesses. For forty days, Miss Marge drags herself out early to serve up hot coffee and the fried egg special to a restaurant full of strangers. R & R regulars can't find a seat—not for breakfast, lunch, or dinner. And Handman's IGA has a constant stream of old men who duck in for bottles of Coca-Cola and packages of bologna for their white-bread sandwiches. Even Miller's Hardware benefits from the races. Mr. Miller can't keep enough saddle soap on hand when the horses are running, or braided rope either. Every business in Shortstop is overrun with customers, like Noah's flood, as Daddy and GramZees joke.

True, some people make a lot of money from the forty days and nights of extra business, but not everyone is pleased to have the races in Shortstop. The straight-talking Rev. Adams is against them. Dead set against them. I find this out from Jimmy on Thursday afternoon after Girls' Night. Mom, GramZees, and I pushed our outing past midnight, and I'm still a little groggy, but Mom came home a winner. She put down two dollars on You-Bet-Your-Life, and the black beauty of a pacer came in first. Jimmy and I are standing in the garden, and I'm telling him all about Mom's win.

Since neither of us could snag any cigarettes, and it's not apple season in the worn-out orchard, we are searching the garden for something to take with us to our hideout. "You know, doncha, that the Methodist preacher's started a campaign to run the racetrack out of town?" Jimmy asks when I finish the story.

"Why would he do that?" I ask in an outraged tone. I am stunned. I stand up holding a shiny green pepper for Jimmy's inspection.

"Thinks gamblin's a bad influence on the young, the old, and everyone in between, I guess." I have more questions, but Jimmy's done with the race talk. He just nods his approval of the pepper, and we head out for our hideout. Roscoe follows along with us in his cat kind of way. He races ahead, then lags behind to track some unseen prey, then races past us again. No amount of calling or coaxing will get him to do what we want. The you'll-never-control-me cat is an interesting distraction, but I'm still thinking about the preacher and his nix on the races.

"He's a Methodist," is Mom's short answer when I ask her about it. I've been pondering the question since Jimmy's revelation this afternoon, so I bring it up over supper. "The Methodists are against gambling...*and* beer drinkin'," Mom adds with a quick glance at Daddy. My dad likes his beer, and my mom likes to needle him about it. Daddy grins. I ignore the exchange. I've got more I want to know.

"Do the Catholics want to stop the races too?" St. Augustine Catholic Parish is the other church in town, but as far as Jimmy knew, Father Michael, the priest, has never said anything against the races. But I'm curious, so I put the question to Daddy.

"Nah," he chuckles, "the Catholics *like* to gamble... *and* drink beer." He smiles and winks at Mom. "Maybe we should be Catholics," he adds with another grin and a second wink. Mom just shakes her head.

I'm quiet. The conversation has put a sick feeling in my stomach. I'm getting sorrier and sorrier I ever agreed to go to the youth fellowship meeting. I see now that I come from a family of gamblers and beer drinkers, which I guess is bad, at least to the Methodists. If the preacher knows — and he most certainly does, because everyone knows everybody's business in Shortstop — then he surely will want me to account for my family's failings. Sunday night will be a perfect time to question me. No wonder the straight-talker insisted I show up. It's an ambush.

CHAPTER 5

I throw a fit about going to the youth meeting on Sunday night, but Mom makes me. She says a promise is a promise. "Give it a try," she finally says, giving a little. "Then if you don't like it, tell the preacher face to face." That's the end of it in her mind.

So at six on Sunday, I show up at the Methodist church basement to face my straight-talker judge. But to my surprise and relief, Rev. Adams doesn't mention one word about the Baxter family's slide into debauchery. He's just as glad to see me as ever. And even better, he points out that Connie and Carla are at the meeting too. That changes everything. This churchy thing just might work out after all.

Carla and Connie—the Cs—and I have been best friends ever since we had Miss Trasfer for third grade. Miss T. has taught at our school *forever!* And no kid wants to be in her class. But the Cs and I got stuck with her for a whole year. Miss Trasfer is probably forty or maybe eighty, it's hard to tell exactly. She has frizz-brown forty-year-old hair and not too many wrinkles, but she acts ancient. She teeters and shuffles her way through the school day. She's like a sloth. Nothing speeds her up. Her class is always late for lunch, late for recess, late to music class, late, late, late.

So, instead of snapping our way through the multiplication tables like the other third grade classes or re-enacting Washington crossing the Delaware, the Cs and I spent each day waiting. Waiting for Miss T. to make her way to the blackboard. Waiting for her to chalk out words that didn't matter. Waiting to hear her say something interesting. But the waiting never panned out. By three-thirty when the bell rang, every kid in class bolted for the school bus.

Every kid except the Cs and me, that is. We were walkers and had to stay longer until all the buses had left.

Miss T. decided to use our wait time to her advantage. "Idle hands are the devil's workshop," she pronounced, and set upon her duty to keep us safe from said devil and his aforementioned workshop, where "you do *not* want to be, no siree bob." She insisted that our idle hands should empty the trash baskets every day, wash all the blackboards, wipe every desk top, and pound all the erasers until they were chalk-free. While we toiled to stay clear of the devil, Miss T. sat sanctimoniously at her desk and munched on her after-school snack — which, of course, she never offered to share.

After a year of shared misery with Miss Trasfer, the Cs and I became forever friends, and here they are again just when I need them. I spot them across the room. Altogether I see about fifteen kids standing around in groups talking and laughing. I relax. I know everyone. Several kids hover over a Skittles game. Gary Jackson watches his spinner careen around the wood box as it kicks down pin after pin. He'll get a good score. Another group pounds out "Chopsticks" on an upright piano. The Cs are there. I join them just as Connie slides to the center of the bench. She pats the seat for Carla and me to sit down on either side of her. Then she starts to peck out notes on the piano.

For the next hour we all just hang out together in the Methodist basement. There are eight girls and seven boys — eight if you count the preacher, who acts like a kid, but in a good way. He almost wins the Skittles tournament; only Gary is better. And he can play all kinds of fun sing-along songs on the piano. They're not all churchy, and not one of them is about the devil or his workshop or slides toward hell in general.

Around seven, Rev. Adams gets us in a circle to talk about organizing our Methodist Youth Fellowship, or MYF, as he calls it. He says we'll meet every Sunday night from six to eight. The first hour is for fun and the second for our business meeting and program. "I'll come," he says, "but you have to run everything. I've got a short program for tonight, and I'll help you elect officers, but from then on you're in charge."

Connie, of course, is elected president, and Dennis is vice president. It makes sense that they get the jobs. Both of their families are Methodists, so they already know how church stuff works. Besides, Connie is really good at running things, which is an important quality for a president. Carla is voted in as secretary — also a good choice because she is a very responsible note-taker at school — and Dale gets the treasurer's spot, which he reluctantly agrees to when no one else wants the job.

After our new officers take over to run things, Connie calls for "old business," which we don't have since this is our first meeting. Then she calls for "new business," which we have a lot of. Dale points out that our first business should be to raise money so he'll have some to "treasure." Everyone laughs at that. But he is right, so we plan a carwash a week from Saturday. I agree to talk to Arch Adler, who owns the only gas station in town. His garage on Main Street is the best location for the wash. It has lots of in-and-out car traffic and an outside spigot for a hose.

When we're done talking about the carwash, Rev. Adams asks us to turn our chairs to face the wall at the end of the room. "I couldn't find the movie screen," he says while he fiddles with a slide projector, "but the white wall should work. Somebody, get the lights." I figure the Adams family vacation slides are coming. *Yawn. Be nice. Act interested.*

But the first picture is not the Adams kids at the beach. It's a bean field with rows stretching beyond the eye of the camera. Pickers stoop all along each row.

Jeff speaks first when the slide show is over and the lights are back on. "If it's so bad in the camps, why do they keep coming?" The "they" are Mexicans who cross the border to work in the United States. Undocumented workers, Rev. Adams calls them—they don't have papers to be here. Some swim the Rio Grande to cross the border, and that's why they get called "wetbacks." Rev. Adams says the name is disrespectful.

The slide pictures were pretty grim. The camps where the migrant families stay have no running water, no electricity, and no flush toilets. The shack "houses" have dirt floors, or mud, depending on the weather, and some families have to crowd together in tents. They stay until the crop is picked, often weeks at a time, and then move to the next crop that's ready.

"It's back-breaking work," Rev. Adams told us as he flipped through pictures of people, including kids, bent over rows in the field. "The company farms pay less than a dollar an hour."

All that brought us to Jeff's question: "If the pay is bad and the camps are nasty, why do the Mexicans come here? Why don't they just stay home?" I was wondering the same thing.

Rev. Adams takes some time to consider his answer. "The migrants come because they don't have a choice," he finally says. "They have to go where the jobs are. It's the only way to feed their children."

I know about having to go where the jobs are. That's how our family ended up in Ohio. We left our home in North Carolina so Daddy could find work up north. Daddy got lucky with a good paying union job, but it was really hard to pick up and move to a strange place. I bet the migrants would rather stay home in Mexico if they could.

"The big commercial farms in the U.S. want to hire migrants," Rev. Adams goes on. "The Mexicans work hard, and they take a lot less money than they should get because they're desperate. Even the kids and old folks have to work to make enough for the family to survive."

None of us speaks.

"But here's the thing," Rev. Adams says, turning upbeat, "Methodists and a lot of other people want to make conditions better for migrant families. And our MYF group can help."

"How?" Several kids speak up.

"Well, for starters, we can send part of our carwash profits to the church in Texas. The one that sent us the slides," he adds. "They need money to buy extra food and medicine to take to the camps." Rev. Adams smiles, then glances at his watch. "But we need a longer discussion to decide. Unfortunately, we're out of time tonight—guess I got too windy." I like the way he makes fun of himself. "We can think on it more and talk next week."

Connie makes up a prayer on the spot to end our first MYF meeting. I am pretty impressed. She asks God, and the sidekick Jesus, to help the migrant families. We all say "amen" and join hands in a circle—right hand over left. *Some secret Methodist code?* I wonder. Rev. Adams moves to the piano and starts a tune called "Bless Be the Tie that Binds." The church kids know the words, and I try to follow along. As far as I can tell, the song's about standing strong together to help each other and to do something good. Kinda the same as being in the union. Daddy calls it solidarity.

CHAPTER 6

n Monday night, I dream about little Mexican kids. They are stooped over rows of green beans, like in our garden, except the rows go on forever in both directions. The sun blazes down on them, and there's no shade. Some kids are crying, and the boss yells at them to pick faster. I wake upset. I can't get the pictures out of my head all day. When I see the evening paper, it's like the nightmare has turned real.

Daddy reads the *Central Ohio Star* every night. He starts with the main articles on the front and moves through to the end. I usually join him just for the back-page "funnies." But tonight, my eye catches the page-one headline: ***Wetbacks: Hundreds of Alien Workers Rounded Up***. There's a big photo underneath. A long line of worn-out migrant workers in straw cowboy hats shuffles toward a waiting bus. Guards stand watch with their guns drawn. They have the "straw-hats" surrounded and the situation is under control. That seems to be the story.

"Wait, Daddy, I want to read about this." I point to the front page.

"About the Mexicans being deported?" He is surprised by my interest.

"They're workers," I tell him. "The headline calls them Wetbacks, but that's not a nice name. They come here for jobs so they can feed their families. We learned about it at the youth fellowship meeting on Sunday."

"Really?"

"Rev. Adams did a program about migrants in Texas. The whole family has to leave Mexico to come here to work. Even grandmas and grandpas. Little kids too," I add.

Daddy raises an eyebrow.

I keep going. "The workers hardly get paid anything, less than a dollar an hour. But they can't find work in Mexico, so they come north, just like we did when we left North Carolina," I finish in a rush.

Daddy's quiet for a minute. Then he says, "Sounds like those workers need a union." I didn't expect Daddy's comment, but it makes sense. He turns back to the front page and starts reading. "Says here that President Eisenhower has turned the Border Patrol loose to round up and deport Mexicans. Ike calls it 'Operation Wetback'." Daddy uses the president's nickname.

"Yeah, and it's ugly," GramZees puts in, surprising us. "California is one of the places where it started, and we tried to put the brakes to it. Some of us didn't like what was happening, and we hid migrants so la Migra couldn't find them."

"La Mee-gra?" I try to let the Spanish roll off my tongue like GramZees does.

"La Migra," GramZees repeats, "that's what the Mexican workers call the Border Patrol. Anyway, I had a Mexican family stayin' at my house, and I helped them go north and get away." GramZees grins.

"You hid people from the Border Patrol?" I'm astounded. Daddy doesn't say anything, but he's listening closely.

"Yep," GramZees confirms proudly. "Remember I wrote and I told ya I couldn't come to Ohio right away because I was helping a family in a fix? Well, it was a Mexican family. They were tryin' to keep from being arrested, and I hid them at my house. Yep," she says again with satisfaction, "that's one family la Migra never got ahold of. I did my little bit to put a stop to Ike's Operation Wetback."

I shake my head. "But I still don't get it. Why would the president want to get rid of the Mexicans? They're here to work. *Somebody's* got to pick the crops. Why *not* the Mexicans?"

"Because they're not white," GramZees says flatly.

"What?" I blurt. Her answer bewilders me.

"Who do you think is behind this deportation craziness?" I think GramZees is taking off in a different direction. "White supremacists, that's who!" She asks and answers her own question. "Racists! They hang black people and now they're deporting brown people..." She takes a breath to calm herself. "They're deporting Mexicans, Blue, because they're not white."

Daddy's been really quiet, but he finally says, "Well, that's a part of it—not all, but part." He's being careful with his words.

GramZees looks directly at Daddy. "You've seen how the white supremacists operate. You grew up in the South where the Ku Klux Klan lynches Negros. What's happening to the Mexicans is not so different. They're deporting them instead of hanging them, but either way, the racists are getting rid of anybody who's not white."

"You may be right," Daddy finally says, evenly, "but I still think it's more complicated."

"Lynching is about hate," GramZees counters. "And Operation Wetback is too. Hate, plain and simple."

"Does President Eisenhower hate Mexicans just because they're brown?" I jump in.

Daddy takes a deep breath, then slowly blows it out. "I don't know if Ike is a white supremacist or not. He's never said so. And no one can know for sure what's in another person's heart."

"But you can judge them by their actions," GramZees says. She's not letting the president off the hook.

"I agree." Daddy smiles. "But...the president says he has to protect our borders. He says he *has* to throw out the Mexicans because they came here without permission. They're undocumented. That makes them criminals, so they should be rounded up and deported." Daddy raises his eyebrows and looks over his glasses at me. He wants me to consider the other side of the argument.

"If that's true," I ask, "why don't the migrants just get permission?"

"Oh, they try," GramZees jumps in. "They try hard to come the legal way, but it's not easy. It takes months, sometimes years to get approved." GramZees throws up her hands in frustration. "And they mostly get turned down anyway. So..."

"...desperate people do desperate things to feed their families," Daddy finishes. He clearly wants to let the conversation go.

"Congress should do their job and fix this immigration mess," GramZees says, changing gears and backing away from the hot talk too.

"Our MYF is having a carwash to raise money," I tell them. GramZees and Daddy look at me like I have grown an extra head. "It's for the migrant families in Texas. At least some of it is, I hope. We're going to decide at our next meeting," I explain.

"I'm glad," Daddy says, and takes my cue. "I'll be there. Our old car is looking pretty dusty. It could use a good soap job." He turns the page to the funnies.

CHAPTER 7

Daddy is true to his word. On Carwash Saturday, he drives our old Chevy to Adler's Garage where a gang from the MYF soaps, rinses, and wipes every car that pulls up. Our group is enthusiastic if not efficient, and by ten o'clock, we have a line of cars backed up along Main Street waiting a turn. Mr. Adler has set us up in front on the street-side of the gas pumps.

"Keep this lane clear," he says, pointing to the entry way. "You can't be blocking people who just want a fill-up." We do our best, but some cars ease on by without stopping for gas. In the beginning, Mr. Adler fusses at us about losing money, but he finally gives up and goes inside. There is no other gas station in Shortstop, so people who need gas will surely be back when the hoopla is over.

Three of us stand on Main Street waving *CARWASH TODAY!* signs. Carla plants herself at the Norwood Street corner to catch drivers coming through the intersection. Pat stands on the sidewalk by Sparkey's Beer Bar to attract folks coming over the railroad crossing. I am in front of Adler's Garage waving my sign and screaming like a banshee to direct cars into line. It is exhausting and fun. Onlookers think I am crazy, but that is okay because it's all for a good cause. I am determined to raise as much money as possible to support the migrants.

When business slows to zero around two o'clock, we close the carwash and adjourn to the church lawn. Arch Adler is gracious but is clearly glad to be done with us.

"How many cars ya think we washed?" Jeff asks. "Seemed like a million." He is sprawled on the cool grass with the rest of us. We are tired. And we are soaked. We stuck to the car-washing task until quitting time, but then Gary squirted Linda's face and she went after him. Soon it was boys against girls wrestling for control of the hose. Mr. Adler watched without complaint, but finally called a halt when a couple of cars pulled up by the gas pumps.

"We were too busy to count," Carla says to Jeff. She's lying with her head propped behind her arms.

Dale and Connie are huddled to the side counting dollar bills. "I don't know how many cars we washed," Dale says, "but we've got two hundred and twenty-six dollars here." He waves the money envelope proudly. That's huge, we all agree, and way beyond our hopes. Most folks gave extra to help out the new youth group. Mr. O'Brien, the president of the bank, gave us fifty bucks to "get us started," he said.

"Seventy-five percent of two-twenty-six is one hundred sixty-nine dollars and fifty cents for the families," Connie breaks in. She's done some quick arithmetic. "That still leaves almost sixty dollars for the Cedar Point trip."

Our MYF has decided to commit the bulk of our profits to help the migrant workers in Texas, but when the topic first came up under old business at the meeting last Sunday, some kids resisted such a large commitment. Sure, they wanted to help the Mexican families, but they thought the biggest chunk of the carwash money should go to fund a trip to the amusement park at the end of summer. We went back and forth trying to decide how to allocate our profits. Rev. Adams remained silent. It was our decision, and he let us talk it out.

In the end, the group voted to give most of the money to buy extra food and medicines for the families on the border. I could tell Rev. Adams was pleased. And so was I because I helped sway the group. I talked about Operation Wetback and how the workers were being rounded up and deported by the Border Patrol—la Migra.

"They don't even get time to collect up their belongings. They're just snatched and gone." This was disturbing new information for the rest of the group.

What I said brought up some good questions. "What happens to the kids when the Border Patrol takes the parents?" Linda wanted to know. It was a question that I hadn't thought about. The front-page picture in the *Star* just showed men getting loaded onto the deportation buses. Where were the children? Where were the women? Rev. Adams didn't know either, but he promised to find out.

But it seems that questions about migrant kids are not the only questions put to the preacher. On Tuesday night I am surprised to hear Rev. Adams's voice coming through our Philco TV. The screen shows him on Main Street outside the church, and beside him is a local reporter from channel three. I reach over and turn up the volume.

"Preacher, tell our viewers why you have taken a stand against the harness races in Shortstop," the reporter asks, and then shoves the mic into Rev. Adams's face.

"It's not about racing itself," he explains. "It's about the gambling that comes with the races." He speaks directly into the camera. "Betting on horses takes money away from families, especially poor families that need every penny they have to pay the rent and feed their children."

The reporter fidgets and reaches for the microphone. He is impatient to ask another question. But Rev. Adams is not done. "Children suffer if parents gamble their paychecks away." The channel three reporter nods like he agrees. But maybe it's just an act. I'm not sure. "Our town should support activities that help children and families, not hurt them. It's the right thing to do."

The reporter takes back control of the mic and picks up the story. "Despite some opposition, town leaders tell channel three that Shortstop residents want the summer racing tradition to continue."

"Having the races here is good for business in our town." A shot of Mayor Thomas flashes onto the screen. "It's a real boost for our merchants and our local economy," the mayor says proudly.

The reporter ends with snippets called "on-the-street interviews." He walks up to a woman coming out of the IGA with a bag of groceries. She rents out a spare bedroom during the racing season, she says, and is glad to have the extra money. A second woman is headed into the Farmer and Merchant Bank and waves the reporter off. She doesn't want to talk about the races. A tall lanky man outside of Turney's Pool Hall is eager to give his opinion.

"Name's Bobby Jack and I've lived here all my life." He pulls the mic too close to his mouth. I can hear his spit crackle. "Let me tell ya this. The races been runnin' in Shortstop ever' summer for as long as I can 'member." He pauses. The reporter reaches for the microphone, but Bobby Jack holds tight. "This preacher comes in," the man's voice gets hard, "and tries ta run our town. We don't like no outsiders tellin' us what to do." Bobby Jack punctuates his words with a bony finger at the camera. "If the preacher knows what's good for 'im, he'll shut up and stay outta our business." The interview ends. The news shifts to the weather forecast.

I click off the television and go to hoe the corn patch, but no matter how much creeping Charlie I pull up, I can't dig out the unsettled feeling the newscast has left. I mention it to Daddy when we're watering after supper. "I wouldn't worry, Blue," he says. "That's just bully talk. Some men throw threats around to make themselves feel big. The preacher knows how to stand up to it. He's got some people riled, but he can take care of himself."

CHAPTER 8

L ingering worries about Rev. Adams and the bully's threat fade away when Mom's canning takes over our lives. The garden puts out an endless line of produce—green beans, beets, cucumbers for pickles, and especially tomatoes. This summer the tomatoes have come in season earlier than usual, and when they get started, they seem to ripen overnight. No matter how many baskets Daddy and I fill or how clean we pick the vines, shiny red globes hang like Christmas ornaments all over the plants again within a day or two.

"Come winter, we'll be glad to have them in jars," Mom reminds me when I grumble about so many tomatoes. I know she's right. GramZees concurs. My grandma works as hard as anyone on the canning, and her specialty is peeling the skin off the scalded red balls. She can skin and core a bucket of tomatoes like nobody's business.

As if summer canning isn't enough to do, Mom also wants to paint. Every room. Every summer. This year, the front room is her first target.

"Brightens everything, don't you think?" Mom climbs down from the step ladder to survey the pale-yellow sample strip still glistening fresh on the wall. The new color is pleasant, I have to admit. Mom took two days to choose it over ten other possibilities on the paint chart Daddy brought home from Miller's Hardware. She finally settled on Dancing Daffodil. It is lively and bright, but to my eye, Dancing Daffodil isn't much different from the Desert Sand it covers. Desert Sand was last year's choice. But Mom likes to change things and, for her, that's enough reason for new paint.

"Open all the windows," Mom instructs after GramZees and I finish throwing old sheets over the davenport and stuffed chairs in preparation. I set myself to the window task. I know the dangers of cooped-up paint fumes. Mom used to paint during the winter, but Petey, our parakeet, was a sad casualty of that schedule. He keeled over dead in the middle of the night when I was ten. His cage hung in the dining room where Mom had rolled Periwinkle Blue over Hint-of-Peach to "cheer up January." The next morning, Daddy found Petey stiff and hard on the floor of his cage. Periwinkle Blue off-gas was too much for his tiny bird lungs.

We held a quick Petey burial service after school while it was still light. Everyone said a few words over his little lifeless body, and Jimmy even came to pay his respects.

He stood with us at the gravesite with his hands shoved deep into his coat pockets. The garden ground was January-frozen, but we did our best to dig a decent hole for our departed bird. The shovel wouldn't do much, though, and the grave ended up skimpy and shallow. I feared we might see green-feathered bones floating up top in the spring rains, but thankfully Petey was still quiet in his grave when Jimmy and I surveyed the burial spot in March and again in April. But dead Petey convinced Mom to skip January cheer-ups from then on and move the paint job to summer, right when the tomatoes came in.

With the gangbuster garden and Mom's painting frenzy, we don't have time to think much about the races. They drone on like background noise night after night from the fairgrounds without much notice. But that all changes when the Loves call.

The Loves' house sits at the end of Columbia Street next to the fairgrounds gate. Anyone headed to the races passes the Loves' house and their empty half-acre beside it. The extra lot gets full sun all day, and it would make a super garden space, but several years back, the Loves hatched a different plan. They discovered that the half-acre was perfect for parking cars. If they packed them right, they could jam fifty vehicles onto their empty lot. And for some years running, they have done just that during fair week in August. This summer, they decided to expand their business to include the forty nights of harness racing. The potential profits from fifty cars a night at two dollars each — scalper prices, according to Daddy — is too much to resist.

The couple devised a team approach to maximize their take. Mrs. Love waves folks down and collects the two bucks while Mr. Love supervises the actual parking. He wedges cars in without an inch to spare. A fat driver can barely squeeze out by the time Mr. Love is satisfied with the parking job. Not one sliver of real estate is wasted. Space is money.

But a problem quickly emerged with the expanded business model. If Mamma Love stands on the street with the *PARK HERE* sign, and Daddy Love shoehorns cars into the tiny designated spaces, then who is watching the Little Loves for forty nights? That's where I come in.

"We would pay you thirty-five cents an hour," Mrs. Love tells me. Which, by the way, I think is a paltry sum considering their scalper prices. "It would be six nights a week from seven to eleven. You would gross more than eight dollars a week!" She nonchalantly throws in the pro-fessional-sounding jargon. She sees herself as a business person now, and I think she wants to impress me. "That's a tidy profit."

Despite my feelings about their cheapskate offer, thirty-five cents an hour is the going rate for babysitting. With eight dollars a week *on top of* daytime grass-mowing money, I'll be rich by the end of the summer. The Huffy Classic Cruiser is all but bought.

But a stubborn doubt begins to scratch in the back of my brain.

"Seems like a good deal," Mom says when I tell her about it. "Maybe you could earn enough for that new bike you want." Mom knows how I think.

"We'll have to start charging you rent," Daddy teases when I mention it to him.

Both Mom and Daddy give the thumbs-up. But still I hesitate. I can't parse why. I can rake in the bucks off the races just like Mr. Turney at the pool hall or waitress Marge at the R & R. Saying no to that seems like a chump decision. What kid would pass up such a summer windfall?

The Loves are ready for me to take over the evening kiddie care, and they want an answer. I promise to let them know by mid-week and mumble some excuse about Mom needing me at home. I am leaning toward the "you'd be a chump to turn this down" option when I happen by Rev. Adams pulling weeds around the shrubs at the church.

"Hey there, Blue. You having a good week?" he says, hailing me. "I was just thinking about you and Connie. I got a home visit to make, and I need help. Think you girls could give me a hand this afternoon?"

"Sure, I guess," I say, curious. "Just need to ask my mom."

"Great!" Rev. Adams stands up from his weeding. "I'll talk to Connie, and if she says yes, you girls can meet me here at three o'clock. We need to load up the car trunk." The preacher heads into the church without offering more information.

Connie and I show up at three. Rev. Adams is already stuffing groceries into his trunk. "Grab some of those, girls," he says, pointing to the bags still lined up on the sidewalk. "We're making a trip to Mudsock."

Connie and I glance at each other. *"What's in Mudsock?"* Connie silently mouths to me. I shrug a "no clue" reply. Mudsock is a huddle of beaten-down houses, a dry goods store, and an old Methodist church several miles outside of Shortstop. It's a blink-and-you'll-miss-it kind of place. We finish loading the bags and climb into the back seat for the short ride.

On the way, the three of us chat about the MYF car-wash success and the upcoming trip to the Cedar Point amusement park. Rev. Adams steers the car past the IGA grocery and the drug store. We pause briefly at the railroad tracks to do a head-check for trains before crossing over. The tracks run between the post office on one side and Winter's store on the other. You can buy almost anything you need at Winter's. In the rear, Mrs. Winter sells two-for-a-penny candy out of a glass case while Mr. Winter rings up bib overalls from the shelves up front. But we're not shopping for candy or overalls today.

Rev. Adams follows Main Street where it curves left toward the grade school and crosses Cemetery Road. Two summers back, Jimmy and I walked miles of that road and never found any sign of a cemetery. No one I've asked has any idea where the road got its name. The same's true for Mudsock, though there are stories about an early settler getting stuck in the mud and losing his sock when he tried to pull his boot free. But who knows for sure?

Main Street becomes Gallon Road just outside of town where everything turns to country real fast. Corn and wheat fields run on both sides of the road with only an occasional farmhouse or barn in between. A few miles along, we turn right toward Mudsock. A dozen or so houses line the road, and we pull up to one of them. It's a tiny cinder block building with a tumbled-down porch tacked onto the front. I guess someone lives there, though it's hard to imagine.

"We're going in to visit with the Harlan family for a few minutes." Rev. Adams turns in the seat to face us. It's the first specifics he's offered about the Mudsock trip. "Let's grab some things from the trunk on the way up to the door." The preacher is very nonchalant, like he takes bags of groceries to falling-away places every day. Connie and I load up and follow him to the front door. A young woman with a diapered baby on her hip opens at the first knock.

"Preacher." She offers a shy smile and throws open the door to welcome us in. A tall, lean man stands behind her holding a blond, curly-headed toddler on his shoulders. He tips his head in greeting. "Y'all find yourselves a seat." The woman waves a friendly arm toward a lumpy brown couch. If she is surprised to see Connie and me, she doesn't show it. We follow Rev. Adams's lead and place our grocery bags on the kitchen table.

The preacher keeps talking all the way across the tiny room. It eases things some. "Good to see you, Ted, Alice." He nods a greeting at the Harlans. "The baby's getting bigger every time I see him. And is this little Edith?" His eyes twinkle as he holds out his finger to the toddler. "This is Connie and Madeline from our youth fellowship." He turns to us. "I think I mentioned them when I was here last week."

The Harlans smile awkwardly. Connie and I smile back, just as awkward. I am tempted to jump in to set the record straight about my name, but instead I just say, "Glad to meet you."

Connie and I sit gingerly on the broken-down couch, and Edith quickly toddles over to inspect us. Almost immediately she climbs into Connie's lap. I don't know what it is, but little kids always take to her right away. I can see Mrs. Harlan is pleased, and she scoots a wooden chair up close so we can talk easier. Rev. Adams finds a place at the table with Mr. Harlan, and soon the two of them are into a deep, quiet discussion.

Mrs. Harlan relaxes a bit when we ask about the baby. "Name's Teddy," she tells us, "like his daddy." She glances at her husband. "And his gran' daddy," she pauses, "and his great gran' daddy too." She smiles at the little joke. "A lotta Teddys in the family, and now we got one of 'em," she finishes with pride. The conversation loosens some more. Teddy's six months old, she tells us, and "a handful to lug around." Edith's "'bout two," and "gets into ever'thing."

"What grade you girls in?" she asks, turning the conversation to us. "Y'all named Connie and Madeline. Right?"

I take the opening. "She's Connie, but folks call me Blue — like a blue jay. My grandma named me."

"Nice name. Kinda different, but nice," Mrs. Harlan says. And I can tell she means it.

"We're in sixth grade," I tell her. "Well, we just finished the sixth. I guess we're in seventh now, but we haven't started yet," I correct.

Mrs. Harlan glances at the ceiling, thinking. "That's 'bout when I had to quit," she says and looks to her lap. Connie and I go silent. We don't know what to say. Things turn awkward again, but then Mrs. Harlan looks up and goes on. "I sure liked school. And I was doin' right well." She smiles. "But I had to quit." She shrugs in resignation. "My daddy got the black lung. I had to help out," she says matter-of-factly.

I know black lung disease comes from working in the coal mines. Miners breathe in the coal dust, and after a while, they're coughin' up blood, GramZees says. She grew up in West Virginia and she saw a lot of miners die from black lung.

"I took up waitressin' when I was twelve," Mrs. Harlan says. "That's how I met Teddy." Her face lights at the memory. "He's some older 'an me, but we liked each other right off. After a little courtin'…well…we got hitched." She smiles. "Married up too young, my daddy said. We come up here to get us jobs, but Edith come quick. An' little Teddy right after. Now I stay home with the babies."

We wait for more of the story, but instead, Mrs. Harlan switches to, "What ya'll studying in school?" Turns out she is most interested in the books we are reading. We tell her. "They good stories?" she wants to know.

"Mine is," Connie confirms, and looks at me.

"Mine's about hobbits and a special ring," I say. "There's a wizard and some elves. It's really different, but I like it."

"I used to read a lot," Mrs. Harlan says, still smiling,

"but now, it's hard to get a holt of any books." She pats baby Teddy on his back, and he puts out a loud burp.

"Next time we could bring you some," Connie quickly offers. "What do you like? I've got all kinds of books. I can loan you some if you want."

Mrs. Harlan beams. "I'd sure appreciate it. I'm not picky, but I like a good mystery."

"I've got the whole set of *Nancy Drew* books." Connie's excited, then considers, "But they might be a little young for you."

"I don't care. I'd give 'em a try."

I guess being married and having two babies to watch after makes Mrs. Harlan a grown-up. But when I see how her face sparkles, I think she looks just like our girlfriends from school. Calling her Mrs. Harlan seems strange.

Rev. Adams is on his feet by the table, and he and Mr. Harlan are finishing up. "You been able to stay clear of the racetrack, Ted?" They are speaking low, but I hear the tail end of their conversation.

"It's hard, Preacher," Mr. Harlan says, "not gonna lie to ya. But I know I got to. Gambling on the ponies landed us in this fix." Rev. Adams nods. "Lost my job because of it. An' almost lost my family. We appreciate all you're doing to get us straightened out."

Rev. Adams nods again, then switches to another thought. "I got a lead on a good job at the GM plant out off Route 40. Think you'd like making parts for cars?"

"I'd sure like to try." Mr. Harlan grins.

On the way out the door, Rev. Adams promises to

come back, and then he pauses to say, "Friday might be a good time to try for that job, Ted. I can give you a lift over to the GM plant." Then he turns to us. "And maybe you would like to come hang out with Alice until we get back." And just like that, the plan is made. I decide that Rev. Adams is a lot like GramZees. He's good at figuring out how to help people.

We load up and head back to Shortstop where Rev. Adams drops us off by the church. Connie and I consider a quick trip to the R & R for a Coke, but when we peek in the restaurant, we see it's already crowded with folks going for an early supper. We decide to skip the Coke and go our separate ways. On the way home, I make a detour down Columbia Street to the Loves' house.

"Hi, Blue." Mrs. Love swings open the door when I knock. I can hear the little Loves squealing and laughing all the way from the backyard. "The kids filled up the big washtub with water," she explains with a smile. "They're having a great time." We settle in the kitchen where she can keep her eye on the kids through the window.

"I've come to tell you that I decided not to take the babysitting job," I blurt out before I lose my nerve. Mrs. Love's smile vanishes. I rush on, "It's a really good offer, and I'm glad you thought of me, but it just won't work out."

"May I ask why?" Mrs. Love pulls out her business side. "It seems like a fair offer, but we might be able to pay a little more."

"It's not about the money," I say. "Thirty-five an hour is the usual rate."

"I see." Mrs. Love is clearly disappointed. "Then what is it?"

Here comes the hard part. I was hoping she wouldn't ask.

"Well, you see…I met someone. A whole family, really. And they're in a bad way because of gambling…on the races…the horse races." I want that to be enough, but I see that Mrs. Love is waiting for more. "The money they needed for food and other stuff went to bet on the horses," I finish. But Mrs. Love's right eyebrow raises into a question mark. She's still not satisfied with my explanation. I squirm. "I don't want to make money from something that might hurt other people. It's a personal decision." There it was.

Mrs. Love's eyebrow drops to its normal place. "I see," she says again. "All right, if that's your decision, then it is." I know it is time for me to leave.

When I get home, GramZees understands right away when I tell her about my conversation with Mrs. Love. "I'm really proud of you, Blue. You stood up for what you believe."

But Mom doesn't say anything for a while when I mention it to her. Finally, she says, "You know, Blue, a person can enjoy gambling without causing harm to their family." Maybe she thinks I'm judging her. Then she adds, "But it's true that gambling can get a hold on some people." She pauses, thinking about something. "You remember my sister Mildred? The one who lives in Nevada? She almost lost her house because she couldn't stay out of the casinos in Las Vegas. Maybe you did right, Blue." Mom reaches over and gives my arm a squeeze. "Let's get supper started."

Overall, Mom and Daddy don't disapprove of my decision, but they are surprised. Actually, as I think about it, I am pretty surprised myself. I won't have the money to get the new bike, but I feel all settled about it inside.

CHAPTER 9

ummer drifts on, and the tomatoes and green beans just keep coming. Cucumbers too. I have to check the cucumber patch every day. And that's why I am the one to notice the first clue.

On Monday, I count ten long green cukes that are almost ready for pickling. But when I go searching on Wednesday, eight of them have vanished. I search and search — cucumbers are good at hiding — but no amount of leaf-turning produces the missing vegetables.

"Someone's stealing our cucumbers," I tell Mom when I come into the kitchen empty-handed again on Thursday. Another six have vanished.

"Surely not." Mom thinks I just missed them. "Everyone around here has more cucumbers than they want. Who would take them?"

"Maybe it's hoboes grabbing a quick snack when the

train stops to fill up the water tank for the steam engine," GramZees says.

"Could be," Mom says, and I agree.

But on Friday when Daddy and I go to pick tomatoes for Saturday canning, we don't get nearly as many as we think we should. And some ears of corn are gone. "Corn wasn't even ready yet." Daddy examines the empty stalks. "Whoever's taking stuff must be pretty hungry."

The garden thefts continue, and they escalate. We can't be sure, but it seems like peaches and apples have gone missing too. "Maybe it's a gang of thieves," Daddy wonders, half joking. "Maybe they're raiding the whole neighborhood and selling what they steal." On the off chance that Daddy's on to something, Mom checks with Mrs. Gallon and Mr. Turney on either side of us, but neither family has missing produce. Nor do the Micks, Jimmy reports when I ask him. We are stumped. Our garden seems to be the only target.

"Thief must think we don't notice," Mom says over supper. "He'll clean us out if this keeps up." She shakes her head in frustration and then shrugs. I'm not ready to give up so easily. I have a plan, but I have to wait until dark.

After the eleven o'clock news, GramZees climbs the stairs for bed, like every night. Then Mom, and finally Daddy. "Five-thirty comes quick," he says, his usual line as he eases out of the recliner. I've been waiting for them to leave.

I relax in the fat stuffed TV chair to watch *Armchair Theatre* like I do most every night. I start the movie, but instead of settling in with a bowl of ice cream, I creep out the front door and make my way around to the back-yard. Someone's gotta figure out who's stealing from our garden, and I'm the one who stays up late when the thief comes.

Roscoe appears beside me out of nowhere. He's not used to human company at this time of night. He slips along beside me in the dark. Crickets chirp back and forth, but everything else is silent—no cars, no birds, no trains in the distance. The moon's up and bright, which is good and bad. Good, because it gives me a clear view of the garden; but bad because it gives the thief a clear view back at me. I stay low as I move through the shadows and silently find my way to the giant lilac bush. Roscoe comes too. His black fur makes him invisible except for the white splotch under his chin.

I want to get as close to the garden as I can, and the lilac puts me about halfway back. Roscoe sits down on his haunches next to me. He's curious about this human who has invaded his night. A long expanse of moonlit yard stands open between me and the next possible cover.

My eyes adjust to the darkness, and I can see the rows of corn stalks and even the outlines of tomato plants with the hills of cucumber vines to their left. I can also make out the gravel ridge of the railroad bed that rises up at the far end of our lot. *Good. I'll be able to spot the thief coming off the tracks. Thief or thieves.* I am leaning toward Daddy's gang theory, though I am perplexed about why we would be the only target.

The moonlight darkens to shadow, and I bolt to the grape arbor. Perfect. Now I am situated to see comings and goings from all directions. I just have to wait. Roscoe waits with me.

We both wait...and wait...and wait...and wait.

Well, this is dumb. I squirm. *I'm hiding in the grapes like a cricket while I could be eating strawberry ice cream.* Roscoe is distracted too. He crouches, ready to pounce on some animal I can't see. I wait a bit longer, then decide to give it up for the night. It was a stupid idea anyway. Maybe the movie is still on.

"Woof!" I hear Bess's short friendly hello. I know her bark. Roscoe does too. His ears twitch toward the sound, but he's not worried.

"Woof!" Barkey joins her greeting. *You just figured out I'm here? Some watch dogs you two are.* I strain to make out their outlines in the darkened dog pen. At first, I don't see the beagles. But then I do.

And...I see who's crouched by the pen petting them through the fence.

I am stunned. As I watch, three shadowy figures rise and move silently from the dog pen toward the garden. At the edge of the plowed ground, they spread out as if following a plan. One heads straight to the corn rows. A second toward the tomatoes. The third and smallest goes to the cucumber vines and begins methodically searching through the leaves. I ought to yell at them or something, but I don't.

I have no idea what to say to three kids stealing vegetables from our garden in the dead of night.

I am still speechless the next morning when I peel hot tomatoes alongside GramZees at the sink. Last night's discovery is vivid in my mind, but it doesn't seem real in the light of day. In the pale glow of the moonlight, I watched as the kid-thieves went about their work. The two girls loaded ears of corn and ripe tomatoes into the skirt-baskets they made with their pulled-up hems. The small boy made his shirt into a makeshift carrier for cucumbers. They took their haul to a grassy spot close to the dog pen. It was there the three sat down to have a picnic. I don't know what else to call it. They piled the ears of corn, the tomatoes, and the cukes in the center of their circle and began their raw-vegetable feast. They ate quickly and in complete silence.

About halfway through the meal, Roscoe left our hideout and wandered over to satisfy his curiosity. Or more likely to claim his share of the attention. He walked straight to the little boy who reached out his hand immediately to scratch the cat's ears and stroke his coat. Satisfied, Roscoe moved on to rub against the girls, each in turn. Then Roscoe — our uppity Roscoe — settled down between the girls to collect his full due of affection. Oddly, Bess and Barkey came to sit silently beside the kids just on the other side of the fence. I suspected this was not the first picnic they had all shared in the middle of the night.

After the vegetable haul was devoured, the biggest girl made her way to the apple tree. She picked some low-hanging fruit, then turned to the nearby peach tree. While she picked dessert, the younger kids cleaned up. All the corn husks and other leavings went into the burn barrel by the dog pen where the scraps would not be discovered. When the fruit-gatherer returned, all three kids paused to pat Bess and Barkey through the wire fence and give Roscoe one last stroke, then they disappeared into our abandoned tool shed like shadowy ghosts.

How can I possibly tell this bizarre tale to my family? I hardly believe it myself.

"You stay up late, Blue?" GramZees shakes me from my thoughts. She shifts her eyes from the sink full of tomatoes. "*Armchair Theatre* was showing a Charlie Chan movie, I think."

"Yep, it was Charlie Chan." I keep my attention on the tomato in my hand. I hope she doesn't ask plot details, seeing as how I never actually watched the movie.

She looks at me full-on, waiting for more, I think. "You're quiet this morning," she says finally, then lets it go.

I work all morning in the kitchen with Mom and GramZees, but I never mention last night's moonlight caper in the garden. By lunchtime, I've pretty much convinced myself that it was all just a dream. By supper I'm not thinking about it at all, and the normal evening routine takes over.

After the eleven o'clock news, everybody else heads up the stairs while I settle in for the *Armchair* feature movie and an especially big bowl of ice cream. I am deep into a creepy story about a scientist who stumbles onto a flying saucer hidden in a forest. He suspects aliens from outer space are invading the earth, so he calls in army guys to check things out. The music builds…a jump-scare is coming. I'm ready.

"S…C…R…EEEEEE…C…H…!" I bolt upright. Not what I expected. And not from the TV. I don't have a clue. But the WHOOSH that follows gives it away. *Someone just flushed the commode.* I relax and return to the movie.

But the WHOOSH keeps WHOOSHING. *Too long for the toilet. Faucet leak?* Maybe… Sigh. Military guys are circling the creepy spaceship. Water's still running. *Gotta check the tap. Maybe I left it running. So annoying.* I sprint to the kitchen.

The sink faucet is tight and dry. But the steady WHOOSH sound is louder. *Maybe a leak in the basement?* I move toward the door that leads downstairs. *S…C…R… EEEEEE…C…H.* Much louder than before…then… dead silence.

And now I know. I recognize the sound. Someone just shut off the spigot — the one outside under the kitchen window. The one that feeds the garden hose.

CHAPTER 10

By morning I have a plan. I'm eager to get my investigation in motion, but that can't happen until tonight. The day drags on and on. Late in the afternoon, Jimmy suggests we go flatten pennies on the tracks, but I don't want to risk hanging around so close to the tool shed. I convince him to go bike riding instead.

"They're building a new house off Cemetery Road. Let's go have a look." Building anything new in Shortstop is a big deal, so I figure he'll want to investigate. I am right. We ride our bikes over to the house-in-progress and spend the rest of the afternoon watching carpenters nail up studs. Little by little, we begin to make out the shapes of the different rooms in the house.

The workers finally call it quits for the day, load their toolboxes into the back of their pickups, and take off. Jimmy and I are inside the house by the time their tailgates are out of sight. We wander around the downstairs first. "This'll be a bedroom." Jimmy points to a small almost-room at the back of the house. The upright studs form the outline of the walls, the doorway and the window openings, even the closet. "And this one's the bathroom for sure." He nods toward the plumbing pipes coming up through the floor in a room off to the side of what looks to be a hallway. I am already on the ladder that leads to the second floor. The upstairs has the outline of two bedrooms, one in the front and one in the back of the house. I am careful not to step through the open hole where the stairs will be.

"Pretty cool up here," I call down. "C'mon up," I coax. Jimmy hates to climb. It's a new thing. He got afraid after he fell out of a tree and broke his arm about a year ago. It takes a while to convince him, but he finally edges his way up the ladder to join me.

It's like being in a treehouse. We watch the tops of cars pass by on Cemetery Road and ogle a couple of old men walking by headed toward town. We don't recognize them and decide they might be "boys" from the racetrack. They don't even know we are there, so it's like we are invisible. "Yep, cool!" Jimmy begins to relax. He drops flat to the floor and scooches to the edge so his head hangs over to the outside. I do the same so part of me is inside the almost-house and part is out. We hang like that for a few minutes, then Jimmy stands. He searches around for scraps of wood scattered in the sawdust. When he collects a good supply, he brings over a stack and we try dropping them over the side two at a time. We experiment to see which one hits the ground first, and then we compare the dropping time of wood chunks to bent nails. Jimmy and I keep experimenting with all kinds of different stuff until it's almost dark. Finally, he says, "Guess we better go. We can't see it hit the ground anymore." We're reluctant to leave the fun, but finally abandon our perch and head out. I've almost forgotten about what waits at home.

When we get to my house, I drop my bike in the front yard and Jimmy pedals up the sidewalk toward his house. Even before I go inside, I can tell Mom has made a pot of pinto beans and baked cornbread for supper. I smell the warm buttery bread when I step on the front porch.

The evening unwinds like usual—eat supper, do up the dishes, feed the dogs, head off Roscoe's "feed me" nips, read the funnies, and chatter about the day. Over supper, Mom mentions that some peppers have gone missing. "I've been waiting for them to turn red. Guess someone else was watching them too." She shrugs. She's given up trying to figure it out.

Daddy says they got a big contract at the shop to make parts for the new Ford pickup trucks coming out at the end of the summer. "There's going to be plenty of overtime work this fall," he says. "Looks like a good Christmas." He smiles at the prospect.

GramZees got a letter from a friend in California. "It's getting worse and worse," she tells us. "La Migra's doing raids in the fields. More and more families are hiding. Some are even hopping trains to get away." GramZees shakes her head. "Don't know why they can't just let folks be."

When it's my turn, I come close to a confession about the kids in the shed, but instead decide to talk about the new house they're building out on Cemetery Road.

When the eleven o'clock news is over, I have *Armchair Theatre* on like usual, but I'm not watching. I am waiting. I'm not even interested in ice cream. Around midnight, I slip out the front door and creep along in the shadows to the backyard. The moonlight is not as bright as before, but it's enough for what I have come to see. I hide in the grapes with the crickets again, but Roscoe's a no-show. After a while, I hear Bess woof. I know the show is about to begin.

The shed door opens wide, and the three kids file silently out. They crouch by the dog pen to greet the beagles, then the scene unfolds as before, but this time I notice details I missed the first time. The kids are thin, really thin. The oldest girl's dress hangs on her rail-like body. She might be twelve, about my age, but she's so slight, it's hard to tell. The middle girl is a head shorter — eight, maybe — and the smallest is the boy. I'd guess he's around five.

I watch as the three go through the nightly routine to gather vegetables, devour their harvest, clean up evidence, and quickly go back inside the shed. Questions stew in my head: *Where did they come from? Why are they hiding? What happened to their parents?* After a second night of watching, I am still no closer to the answers. The only thing I am sure of is that they need help.

I spend the first half of the night surveilling the shed situation and the second half sleepless in bed, trying to figure out what to do about it. By morning, I haven't come up with a full solution or one that's even close, but I have decided on a next step: I have to get the kids some more substantial food. They must be really hungry; raw corn and a few tomatoes night after night is not nearly enough, and from the looks of them, they've been going without for a while. It's a big risk to leave food for them because they will know someone has found them out. They might just run, but I am hoping against hope that they won't.

I've decided what I need to do, but like yesterday, I have to wait till night to get to it. GramZees, Mom, and I spend another day in the hot kitchen canning vegetables. This time it's green beans instead of tomatoes. My job is to help GramZees wash, string, and snap the bean pods. Mom takes over from there and gets the beans into quart jars and pressure-processes them in her big canner.

GramZees and I sit at the table with a huge pile of just-picked beans in the middle. Stringing and snapping is an okay job, and normally I enjoy the chance just to sit with GramZees and talk. When she gets started, she can tell some funny stories about growing up in the "hollers" of West Virginia.

"I wailed the tar outta Virginia, and Mommy had to pull me off..." GramZees is deep into one of my favorite tales about how she outsmarted one of her eight sisters. Normally I laugh big when GramZees tells the end part—she makes it better every time. But today, I'm not picturing GramZees hiding in the outhouse fifty years ago to catch her sister. Instead, I'm seeing three kids crouching in our dark tool shed right now.

"What are you studying on, Blue? You're off in another place this morning." GramZees has stopped her storytelling and is staring hard at me.

"Oh, sorry, GramZees," I jerk and quick-smile. "Just not awake yet. Couldn't get to sleep last night. Must've been something I ate."

"Maybe so," she says, but her eyes tell me she's not swallowing my explanation.

We finish the canning by two, and twenty-one quarts of green beans line the counter to cool and seal. "We'll be eating from the garden all winter," Mom says as she admires the day's output. After we wash all the canning paraphernalia and get it stored in the cabinets, we each drift away. GramZees goes up to take a nap, and Mom settles in her rocking chair to watch an afternoon soap opera on channel six. I head to the garage to find one of Daddy's burlap bags. I've decided it will be just the right thing to use for tonight's food delivery.

I muddle through the rest of the afternoon and evening, waiting for the eleven o'clock news to finally fade to *Armchair Theatre*. I have a moment of panic when GramZees doesn't take to the stairs with Mom and Daddy. "Think I might watch the movie with you tonight, Blue," she says. "I'm not sleepy yet. Guess I took too long a nap this afternoon." She looks straight at me for my reaction.

"Well...sure, GramZees...uh...that would be...great," I stutter. She sits for a moment as if she's thinking something over.

"Oh, on second thought, maybe I'll just go on to bed,"

she finally decides. "We got an early day tomorrow. You and your daddy made sure of that." She chuckles at the last part. She means the whopper basket of lima beans on the back porch. "And besides, I've seen the movie already." GramZees usually doesn't mind watching movies over again. She says that she gets more out of it the second time, so I am a little surprised when she decides against it. But I am relieved.

I'm antsy for the upstairs bedtime noises to settle, and when I finally hear Daddy's first snore, I force myself to wait an extra fifteen minutes just to be sure. I retrieve the burlap bag from under the couch where I've stashed it and move quietly to the kitchen to fill it up. Roscoe follows me from the front room and stations himself by the icebox. His cat radar is in high gear. He senses something interesting is in the works. The trick is to get enough food to do some good for the hungry kids in the shed, but not so much to draw Mom's attention to the missing items. I decide on a package of sliced cheese, three peanut butter and jelly sandwiches, and a quart of milk—which is risky because Mom might notice the milk. At the last minute, I throw in a container of cooked rice and pinto beans along with some leftover cornbread. I remember spoons, glasses, a gallon jug of water from the tap...and a note.

My plan is to go straight to the shed with the bag and hang it on the handle. All day, I debated whether to say something through the door when I deliver the food, but I decided instead to attach the note to the burlap. It reads: *Don't be afraid. This food is for you. Please eat it. Your friend, Blue.* I have kept the message simple, and I hope it's friendly sounding. I don't want the kids to bolt and run, but I know it's a risk.

For this trip, I don't bother sneaking around in the shadows. I head directly toward the garden. Roscoe trails along to see what's up. The night is clear and bright, and I find my way easily. I loop the burlap bag over the door handle, and then I leave. Roscoe loses interest and melts into the darkness on his nighttime cat business. I'm purposefully noisy on the way back, and I even let the back screen slam a little as I go into the house. I hope it's enough to convince them I've left.

But that's not my real plan. After a few minutes of watching through the kitchen window, I ease back outside and slip silently through the shadows to the grape arbor.

It takes a while before the kids come out—way past their usual time to raid the garden. I begin to fear they've gone, but finally I hear Bess's quiet woof. My eyes strain to see. I can make out only the oldest of the three. She is standing outside the shed door staring at the bag I've left. I hope she sees the note. The girl looks all around before she slips the knot loose and peers inside to examine the bag's contents. She makes one last glance around, then opens the shed door again. I think she's going back inside, but then I realize she is telling the others to come out. She's decided it's safe.

The three skip the garden raid and go straight to the picnic. They sit in a circle and go through the bag together. The oldest divides the sandwiches and spreads the other food out to share. The container of rice and beans gets passed around so everyone gets some. For the first time ever, I can hear the kids whispering to each other as they eat. I can't pick up the words, but I can tell they are not speaking English.

When the picnic is over, they hang the limp bag on the door handle and retreat back inside the shed. Before the oldest steps through the door, she takes one last look around. Her stare settles on the grape arbor. She has figured out I am there.

When I'm convinced that the three kids have settled back into their hideout, I move silently toward the house and slip through the back door into the dark kitchen.

"What were you doing outside, Blue?" GramZees's firm, quiet voice startles me. I see her silhouette at the kitchen table. She's been waiting for me.

CHAPTER 11

I spill out the whole tale to GramZees as we sit in the dark kitchen whispering deep into the night. I tell her about my nighttime surveillance that led to the startling discovery. I describe the kids as best I can, including how the oldest girl watches over the younger ones like a mother. I tell GramZees about the moonlight picnics by Bess and Barkey's pen, and how the beagles don't give the kids away. "It's like the dogs know to keep silent," I say. "Even Roscoe's in on it." I describe how our cheeky cat has befriended the garden "thieves."

"Seems our pets know more about what's going on around here than we do," GramZees whispers. I can tell she's smiling. I end the story with the burlap bag filled with food, my note, and how I think the kids speak another language. "And I'm pretty sure the oldest girl spotted me hiding in the grapes," I finish.

GramZees is silent, and for a long moment I'm afraid she doesn't believe my preposterous story. Her first question surprises me: "Do you think the children were speaking Spanish?"

"Maybe," I respond slowly, "but I couldn't hear them very well, and even if I did, I might not know. I don't speak Spanish."

"You don't, but I do. At least some," she adds. "Hopefully enough." Then I know GramZees has figured something out. "The children might be Mexicans hiding from la Migra," she says carefully. "But where are their parents, and how on earth did they end up here?" These are questions we cannot answer yet.

GramZees and I talk a while longer to decide what we should do next. "Nothing tonight," she says. "If the kids are who I think they are, they'll stay put for now. They've got nowhere else to go."

That decided, we discuss when to tell Daddy and Mom. In the end, we opt to keep the secret between us, at least for now. "Knowing about this could put your folks in a hard spot," GramZees explains. "They'd have to report it. It's against the law to help folks hiding from la Migra."

GramZees is silent for a moment, thinking it through one more time, then says, "No, best not to bring your mom and daddy into it until we have to." I agree reluctantly. I'm bothered about keeping such a big secret from my parents, but I am relieved that at least GramZees knows. This secret is too heavy for me to carry alone.

"You handled this good, Blue. Real good." GramZees reaches for my hand. "Let's get some sleep." She yawns and stands up. "Nothing more we can do tonight. But tomorrow," she whispers as we walk from the kitchen, "we need to make a visit to the tool shed."

———————————

Both GramZees and I are up early even though we had a short night. After breakfast, we huddle together by the apple tree out back. Mom thinks we're looking for apples to fry up for supper.

"We got us a break." GramZees talks softly as we scour the ground for fallen apples that are still good. "Your mom and daddy are leaving right after supper to drive into Columbus for a movie. Your mom wants us to clean up the dishes so they can get on the road early. It's a double feature, so they won't be back till close to eleven."

This *is* a break. Daddy and Mom hardly ever go out. Now GramZees and I can visit the shed as soon as it gets dark and no one will be suspicious. "We should take more food," I say under my breath—not that anyone could hear us this far from the house.

"And water," GramZees adds. "Maybe some cookies too." She grins. "I 'spect any kid can use a cookie, even kids who are hiding out. Maybe especially the ones in hiding." She chuckles. "I'll whip up a batch of chocolate chip this afternoon." We have our plan.

After lunch I walk uptown to meet Connie and Carla for ice cream at Willie's. Carla says there's a new flavor called Lemon Zest that we ought to try. After a sample taste, I skip the Zest and go with a Dark Fudge bottom and Mint Chocolate Chip top. The Cs get the Lemon topped with Orange Creamsicle. We decide to take our cones for a walk past the school. "We can go the circle," Connie suggests, "Main to Cemetery to Norwood. That should get us back to the church in time for the bookmobile."

We stroll the mile-long route and talk about how our summers are going. Connie's taking her 4-H Holstein to the state fair. The cow is at her grandpa's farm outside of town, and she goes every day to tend to it. "It's a lot of work," she says. "I'm not sure I'll do it again next year. I know, I know, I always say that," she adds with a chuckle. "But when the calves come in spring, I get the urge again." She shrugs. "So, I must like it, or maybe I'm just a glutton for punishment." Carla and I just listen. We've heard this all before...last summer...and the summer before.

Carla tells us she started swimming lessons at the Shaunee Hills pool and she really likes it. "Lots of cute boys at the pool." She grins. We meander past the school building, which reminds us that our summer's going by fast, which in turn reminds us of the MYF trip to Cedar Point and how much fun we're going to have. I mention that I turned down the babysitting job at the Loves', and they're not sure I made the right decision.

"But you won't get the new bike," Carla wails.

"I know, but I'm still glad, and that's what counts," I say with confidence. I am bursting with the news about the kids in the shed, but I zip my lips.

We pass a big two-story house on Cemetery Road that went up for sale last year after ole man Blackledge died. We notice that the "For Sale" sign is gone and someone's cut the grass. "My mom says a Negro family bought it." Connie flips her thumb toward the house as we pass. "And she thinks they have a boy who'll be in our class next year."

Carla and I are both surprised by the news. Shortstop is pretty much an all-white town except for the Washington family that lives in a tiny house at the corner of Madison and Cemetery. They keep to themselves, though, so it's kinda like they're not really here at all. Daddy thinks the Washingtons act like the Negroes in North Carolina. The black people there don't want to draw attention to themselves, he said, so the Ku Klux Klan won't take notice of 'em. According to Daddy, if the Klan thinks a Negro is "gettin' uppity," it's dangerous for them, what with the lynching and all. I'm not sure why the Washingtons stay to themselves in Shortstop. It doesn't seem dangerous here, but who knows. Maybe they know stuff I don't.

"Why do you suppose the Negroes are moving here?" Carla's question is not mean, just curious. "I feel sorry for that new boy. I sure wouldn't want to be the only black kid at school. Who would you hang out with? You just wouldn't...fit in." Carla thinks out loud.

"Why not?" I blurt. I'm surprised by how mad I sound. "It doesn't matter what color people are, or where they come from," I add fiercely. "Everybody's the same inside, and they should get treated the same." Then I realize I'm not talking about the new family moving in. I'm defending the Mexican kids hiding in the shed. The Cs have gone quiet. They can tell something's hit a nerve in me, but they can't figure what.

The bookmobile lumbers past and breaks the tense moment. It takes the turn onto Norwood Street, and we tear into a dead run for the church. By the time we arrive, we're three shiny sweat balls and seriously out of breath. Rev. Adams is already in line ahead of us, but he drops back to talk. "You girls are coming next Sunday night, aren't you? We've got a bunch of planning to do to get ready for the Cedar Point trip. And I just picked up a letter at that post office from the folks in Texas." He pats an envelope in his front shirt pocket. "They said the money we sent for the migrant families really helped a lot."

The line moves quickly, and our conversation ends at the bookmobile door. I already know what books I'm looking for, and I go straight to them when I get inside. *How to Speak Spanish in Ten Easy Lessons* is on the bottom shelf next to the *English-Spanish Dictionary*. I check out one copy of each.

CHAPTER 12

When I get home, dozens of chocolate chip cookies are piled on wire racks lined up across the counter. "Think you made enough?" Mom teases GramZees when she comes into the kitchen from the front room. "My land, what are we going to do with all these?" She takes stock.

"Don't worry. I'm pretty sure they'll get eaten." GramZees flicks a quick grin at me. "Why don't you give 'em a taste, Blue, to see if they're passable."

"I thought you'd never ask." I wink and snatch the nearest cookie. I pronounce it "excellent" and suggest I probably need another one to be sure. But Mom says it's too close to supper, so instead I begin stacking the crispy goodies into the fat cookie jar. The broken ones are fair game, I decide.

"Put the extras in this." GramZees hands me a large Tupperware container. Again, she gives me a sly grin.

After supper, GramZees and I are eager to get Mom and Daddy on their way to the movies. "Go on, you two. Blue and I've got this." She means the dirty dishes. It doesn't take much encouragement to get the movie-goers gone. GramZees and I quickly finish the cleanup and start packing the night's food gift into the burlap bag. The big container of cookies goes on top. At dark, we walk out the back door toward the shed. Roscoe slips out the door with us.

Bess greets us with a tail-wag, and Barkey woofs and jumps excitedly on the fence. Oh well, good thing we weren't trying to sneak up in surprise. GramZees goes to the shed door and knocks softly. She speaks quietly through the door, "Hola, mis amigos." (Hello, my friends.) "Queremos hablar." (We want to talk.) I can mostly understand GramZees's simple phrases or at least guess at them.

At first, we don't hear anything inside the shed, and I fear that the three occupants have fled after all. But then the door slowly opens, and we see the oldest girl standing in the dark shielding the two younger ones behind her.

GramZees speaks softly again. "No tengan miedo. Queremos ayudarles." First, GramZees tells them not to be afraid. I get that part, but I'm a little lost after that. I think she says that we want to help.

GramZees goes on: "¿Podemos entrar?" I'm not sure what she asked, but the door opens wider and the girl stands aside to let us in. She closes the door behind us and we all stand silently in the dark shed.

Well, someone has to say something, I think, so I start. "Mi nombre es Blue," I say softly. I practiced introducing myself while GramZees and I washed dishes tonight. I'm pretty proud of myself.

"Me llamo Abuela." GramZees has decided to just call herself Grandma — Abuela in Spanish. The name GramZees seems too complicated to explain. Now it's the girl's turn.

"Soy Dolores." The oldest girl points to herself. We can barely see each other in the thin light, but my eyes are adjusting. "Su nombre es Elenita." She smooths the other girl's long dark hair. "Y él es César." She pulls the little boy close. Then she surprises us. "I speak English a little," she says shyly.

The conversation begins. Half in Spanish and half in English. I try to follow as best I can. GramZees translates when I don't understand the Spanish or Dolores doesn't know all the English words. We're just getting into the story when we hear scratching at the door. Everyone freezes. The scratching starts again. "Oh. Sólo es el gato," Dolores whispers in relief. "It is just the cat," she repeats in English. She stands to open the door a crack. Roscoe slips into the shed and promptly sashays to César's side and flops down. As we start up the talk again, the kids open the food bag. Their eyes get big when they see the cookies. It's the second time I've seen them smile. The first was when Roscoe appeared.

GramZees starts with the obvious question. "¿Cómo llegaron aquí?" (How did you get here?)

It's a long story. Dolores sighs, and starts at the beginning. She tells us that her whole family comes from Mexico every year to work in the Texas fields. The family includes her mom, dad, the three kids, and her grandma. They come in March when the strawberries are ready to pick, and then they move on to blackberries and blueberries. Everybody works, Dolores tells us, even little César who is only five.

"All the time, the boss yells 'Faster! Faster!'," Dolores explains what it is like. "Mi papa dice que el jefe sólo sabe una palabra — the boss only knows one word," she translates. All the kids laugh when Dolores repeats their father's joke.

It is hard to pick all day, Dolores, says. "It is very hot," she explains. "The boss does not give us much water. And we are not allowed to stop. 'Faster! Faster!" she mimics the boss again. "Pero así son las cosas." She shrugs.

"But that's the way things are," GramZees says in English.

"Sin trabajo, sin dinero. No work, no money." Dolores shrugs again.

"This summer starts the same – we pick, they pay — but then it changes." She hesitates. Glances at Elenita and César. "The police come to the fields."

"La Migra?" GramZees asks.

"Sí, la Migra," Dolores confirms. "They chased us. We ran. We got away, but many others? No. La Migra had guns." Dolores makes her hand into a pistol to show us. "They took everyone who did not escape, even the kids. Many were our friends, and we do not know what happened to them." She reaches out to Elenita and César and pulls them closer. "We wanted to work, but after that we were afraid. Then it got even worse. Papá told us la Migra went to…" She turns to GramZees. "Campamento de migrantes, how do you say in English?"

"Migrant camp," GramZees says. "You mean the place where migrant workers live?"

"Sí, Papá told us la Migra went to one of the camps at night with guns when people were asleep. They rounded up everyone! ¡Todos!" Dolores sweeps her hand to say they took everyone. "They put the mamás and papás on one bus. The kids on another one." Dolores holds out her right hand, then her left, to show how the kids and their parents were separated and put on different buses. "Los niños ya no ven a sus papás."

"The kids didn't see their moms and dads again," GramZees repeats. Crickets chirp outside the shed, but we are all quiet. Roscoe has stopped purring.

Dolores finally speaks again, "After that, Mamá and Papá said we must leave."

The family decided to come to Ohio to get away from la Migra, Dolores tells us. "Nuestra abuela vive en Ohio," she says in Spanish as she throws a quick smile to Elenita and César. "Our grandma lives in Ohio now," she translates. That news surprises us.

"What is your grandma's name?" I ask. GramZees translates.

"¡Abuela! Claro." Grandma! Of course. All three answer at once. Smiles all around.

Dolores goes on, "This year, Abuela did not stay in Texas with us. She went to pick rábanos and lechuga in Ohio." Dolores stops. "How do you say rábanos and lechuga in English?" Dolores turns to GramZees.

"Radishes and lettuce," GramZees tells her.

"She went to pick radishes and lettuce in Ohio. Melard... Ohio." Dolores takes time to think of each English word. "There is a big farm there, and Abuela can work all year." Dolores explains. "A lot of Mexicans live in Melard, and one man, José, he likes our abuela, and she likes him too." Dolores flashes a quick smile. "So, our abuela stayed in Melard to work and to be with José." Dolores pauses., "When the trouble started in Texas, Abuela called Mamá and Papá." Dolores holds a pretend telephone to her ear. "She told them to come to Melard. She said there is no Migra there, and it is safe for Mexicans."

"So, we ride a boxcar train from Texas to Ohio." Dolores explains simply, using one hand to mean Texas and the other for Ohio. "We try to get to our abuela. But... we get here instead.," Dolores drops her head in disappointment.

There are still lots of questions. What happened to their mom and dad? How did they get separated? But the answers can wait. For now, GramZees and I at least have the basic story. Dolores looks exhausted. We are sitting on the floor with our backs against the shed wall. Elenita leans her head on Dolores's shoulder. She's droopy-eyed. César's head is in Dolores's lap, and he has gone to sleep. Roscoe snoozes next to him.

"No more talking tonight," GramZees decides. "No hablen más esta noche." We stand to go.

We want to get the kids into a better place, but for now the shed will have to do. Before we leave them for the night, we go to the house and haul back a stack of thick blankets to fold into makeshift mattresses. At least they can have a softer bed. We also bring towels, soap, and extra jugs of water. Dolores wants to get everyone cleaned up. And of course, we bring more food for tomorrow. The family has missed a lot of meals.

"Buenas noches, nuestros amiguitos — Good night, our little friends." GramZees and I gently hug Dolores, Elenita, and César one at a time as we say good night and get ready to go back to the house.

"Gracias por todo." Dolores slips into Spanish to say her final thank you. "Good night, Blue. Good night, Gram...Zees." Dolores tries out the name. GramZees suggested the change.

GramZees and I walk slowly toward the back porch and take a seat on the swing. My head is spinning from all that we heard. When Mom and Daddy get home, they are surprised to find us still sitting on the back porch. "What are you two doing out here in the dark?" Mom asks. "Thought you'd be watching the movie on TV." We mumble something about it being cooler on the porch and follow them inside, then up the stairs to bed.

CHAPTER 13

 good night's sleep clears our heads some, but we're still not certain what to do next. Finally, I suggest that we make a list.

"First, we should find a better place for the kids to hide," GramZees says, "before someone gets suspicious about the shed. Besides it's not very comfortable, to say the least." I agree.

"We've got to find their abuela." I use the Spanish word for grandma. "Maybe she'll know what happened to their mom and dad."

"She probably won't," GramZees says grimly. "I bet la Migra scooped up the parents somewhere along the way. They could be in jail somewhere—anywhere between here and Texas. Or they could be deported...even worse." She leaves the thought unfinished. "Tearing families apart like this is shameful!" GramZees is riled up. "This family may never get put back together again," she says sadly.

"But we can't give up hope," I say quietly. "We have to help if we can."

"No, we can't lose hope, Blue," GramZees responds softly, "and yes, we do need to find a way to help make this right or at least better. Let's put our hearts to it."

"So, where's a better place to hide?" I focus. "And how do we find the grandma?"

We spend time discussing hide-out options, and finally settle on a plan that neither of us likes but seems the only way: We have to convince Mom and Daddy to hide the kids in our house. Tonight, we have to tell them what we know.

Mom outdoes herself with supper. She's made one of Daddy's favorites, fried perch with homemade tartar sauce. There's slaw, too, and thin-sliced crispy fried potatoes. "Mmmm! Mmmm! Good!" Daddy can't stop saying it. Fried perch is one of my favorites too, but tonight it lays heavy in my stomach along with the news GramZees and I have to share.

Before anyone leaves the table, GramZees speaks up. "Can everyone sit still for a while? Blue and I have something we need to tell you."

"Well, this sounds pretty serious," Daddy jokes. He's still feeling good about the meal. Mom stops stacking dirty dishes and looks at us curiously. We've got their attention, so GramZees and I plunge in. It takes a while, but by the end, we share as much as we know: how I discovered the kids hiding in our shed, how GramZees got involved, how I took food from the icebox to feed them, and finally, how three Mexican kids fled from Texas in search of their grandma and ended in up our backyard instead. Daddy and Mom listen in stunned silence. When GramZees and I are done with the telling, neither of my parents says anything. I have no idea what they are thinking.

Finally, Mom says, "Well, we have to do something about this. Those Mexican kids certainly can't stay out there in that shed!" She's adamant. My heart sinks. Her reaction is worse than I feared. She wants to get rid of them — maybe turn them over to the police. Now *I* am speechless.

But Mom goes on. "They absolutely can't stay in that shed! We have to get them into the house! Right now!" I flash my relief to GramZees. "Those poor kids could use a decent meal for sure and a good place to sleep." Mom is on a mission now. She believes that good food and a good night's sleep can solve a lot of problems. She's probably on to something. "Those poor little kids," she says again. She's up from the table and ready to march out to the shed immediately to rescue all three of the hideaways and plunk them down in front of one of her garden feasts.

"Whoa! Whoa! Now hold on a minute." Daddy raises his hand to slow things down. "We gotta think this through. It's not that simple."

"No, it's not that simple," GramZees agrees quietly. "You could be in big trouble if anyone finds out you are hiding the migrant kids here. You could go to jail for harboring them." She says it plain.

Daddy nods. "I thought that might be the case." Mom looks at him askance. She's back in her chair. Daddy holds up his hands to defend himself. "Don't get me wrong. I'm all for helping people—especially kids—but I don't like breaking the law. Harboring these Mexican kids could cause us all a lot of trouble we just don't need to get ourselves involved in."

"We're not 'harboring' them." Mom's voice has a touch of outrage. "We're giving them something to eat and a place to sleep. That's just the decent thing to do."

"Of course, it is," GramZees says slowly, "but doing the decent thing could get you arrested."

"Pshaw!" Mom is getting riled.

"It's true. Listen to your mother. She's got experience in these kinds of things," Daddy pleads. He looks determined. "We could bring the law down on us, and I'm not sure I want to risk it. We could lose everything we've worked for."

"That's a fact." GramZees is definite. She looks at Mom directly. "As far as the law is concerned, those Mexican kids are criminals. They are in this country illegally. And they are running to keep from being deported. You'll be considered criminals too if you don't turn them in." GramZees wants to be sure we understand how serious this is. No one says anything.

Finally, Mom speaks. She is calmer now. "Whatever we do, I think we have to protect those kids. If Blue was alone in a strange place and in a bad situation, I hope and pray someone would help her if they could."

Mom's made her final plea and turns to Daddy. He looks down. I can't see his eyes, but then he raises his head and nods. "I do too," he says quietly. "I would want someone to help her if she was in trouble." He reaches his hands out, one to Mom and one to me. He tips his head to include GramZees. "Okay. Let's do what we can for these kids and protect ourselves as best we're able." I think we made some kind of family pact.

Now that we have decided to invite Dolores, Elenita, and César to stay with us, Mom wants to go get them as soon as we clear the supper dishes. But GramZees advises against it. Now she's the one who wants to slow things down. "We have to wait for dark. This is not just your everyday invite," she teases. "But it's not just that," she says, turning serious. "It's gotta be their decision to move into the house, not ours. We need to talk with them."

"But why wouldn't they want to come?" Mom wants to know. Maybe she's a little offended.

"Oh, they probably will," GramZees quickly assures her, "but you have to remember, these kids have been through a lot, and they have survived by being very careful. They've got lots of good reasons not to trust strangers — especially strangers who are not Mexican."

"I guess you're right," Mom concedes. "I just feel so bad for them, and I want to help." She's clearly disappointed, but we talk it through some more and finally settle on a plan. GramZees and I will go by ourselves after dark around nine. We'll take food, and we'll see then what Dolores and the other two kids think of our offer.

As soon as we clean up the kitchen, we put together the items to go into the burlap food bag. Mom insists on two sandwiches each, plus bananas, and some rice pudding with raisins. She also mixes up a can of frozen orange juice in a quart jar. At the last minute she throws in a big bag of fresh popped corn and a plastic container of chocolate chip cookies—of course. "You feeding an army?" GramZees teases when she hoists the bag.

"Well, if I can't feed them here at the table, at least I can fill 'em up out there in the shed," she says lightly. I pick up a gallon jug of water and we make our way out the back door. Roscoe flips his tail tall like a flagpole and leads the way. He knows the nightly routine.

At our first soft tap, Elenita opens the shed door. César is right behind her. Together we quickly lay out the food Mom has sent, and when there's nothing but cookies left to eat, GramZees begins the serious discussion. Dolores listens carefully as my grandma explains that Mom and Daddy want them to leave the shed and hide inside our house—at least until we can find their abuela. Dolores asks some questions in Spanish that I do not understand, but I can tell she is reluctant. "She's afraid it's a trap," GramZees turns to tell me at one point. Then she goes back to talking Spanish with Dolores. They go at it a long time.

In the end, I don't know what GramZees says to finally convince Dolores that it's safe—that we are safe—but she does. And before we say good night, we have agreed that the move will happen tomorrow after dark.

CHAPTER 14

We're all up early, and after Daddy leaves for work, Mom, GramZees, and I spend a good part of the day getting the house ready for our three guests. Mom suggests I move into GramZees's room and give mine over to our visitors. "All three kids will probably sleep in the same bed," GramZees says. But just in case it's too crowded, I make a special soft place on the floor with a pile of thick quilts. Roscoe tries it out and pronounces it fit for a king—namely, him.

"What do Mexican kids eat?" Mom frets like the good host she is. She wants to fix a hearty supper. No more late-night picnics by the dog pen.

"Well," GramZees replies, "meals are pretty simple in the camps—mostly just pinto beans, chili peppers, and stacks of corn tortillas. Sometimes just tortillas if the family's really poor. Maybe avocados and eggs if they can afford to buy them. Meat? Almost never."

"Oh, my land," Mom says, "the IGA grocery doesn't sell avocados! And even if they did, I wouldn't know what to do with them. And I don't know anything about making tortillas!" Mom's in a tizzy. "What on earth can I fix for them?"

"Make the good food you always make," GramZees says. "Just be sure to have a pot of pintos. These kids have been eating raw corn and cucumbers for days. They'll love whatever you cook. Keep it simple and stop worrying. That's my advice." Mom starts cooking, but she doesn't stop fretting.

Late in the day, GramZees and I make a trip to pull some carrots from the garden—or that's what it looks like we're doing. What we really do is have a quick conversation with Dolores through the thin plank walls of the shed. GramZees explains that she and I will come to get them after it gets dark. "My mom is fixing a special meal," I whisper through the cracks. GramZees translates. I hope that makes them smile.

The trip from shed to house happens without a hitch. Dolores, Elenita, and César are ready and make no sound, not even a whisper, as we fast-walk from their hideout to the back porch. They are experienced in the ways of stealth. Daddy and Mom wait for us in the dark kitchen. All the curtains are closed, and we don't turn on lights until everyone is inside. "No need to take chances," GramZees reminds us.

When the back door is closed, Daddy pulls the string for the overhead light. Mom steps forward to greet the new arrivals. "Bienvenidos, amigos." Mom and Daddy say,

"Welcome, friends" in Spanish just like we have practiced. Everyone smiles.

"Muchas gracias por todo. Thank you for everything," Dolores answers shyly. Everyone stands stiffly, and no one knows what to do next. Then Mom takes charge like the experienced hostess she is. She sweeps her hand toward the table, and with GramZees's help, invites everyone to sit down. Daddy takes the cue and pulls out chairs for our guests. The shuffle to get seated around the table loosens the tension. Sharing a meal seems like a good place to start.

Mom has taken GramZees's advice and kept the meal simple: pintos, cornbread, fried chicken, corn on the cob, sliced tomatoes, cabbage slaw, and fruit salad. The kids' eyes sparkle in wonder. Mom relaxes. Her meal is a hit already. Our guests fill their plates modestly on the first round but go back for more. They eat and eat. Daddy makes his usual joke about kids having hollow legs—and GramZees does her best to translate—but our guests just stare blankly at him. They have no idea that he means they are eating a lot to fill up the empty leg. "Well, guess it gets lost in the translation," he chuckles.

The conversation starts slow because we go back and forth in two different languages with GramZees doing translation as best she can in between. Little by little, though, we all relax, and by the end it doesn't matter so much if we know every word. We discover other ways to "talk" to each other. Elenita's big smile tells Mom the chicken is perfect. César's second ear of corn is all Mom needs to hear. Daddy makes more silly jokes in English and the kids have no idea what the joke is, but everyone laughs. When it's time to clear, Dolores makes motions to help with dishes, but Mom gives her a friendly wave-away.

After supper, I take our visitors upstairs to show them around. Dolores's eyes light up at the bathroom. "¿Podemos bañarnos?" She points to the tub and pretends to wash herself. "We can take bath?" she asks in English.

"¿Baño? Sí." I nod, secretly proud of my Spanish. I lay out towels and show Dolores how to adjust the bath water. The spigots on our ancient tub are tricky. GramZees comes upstairs with some clean clothes Mom found packed away in a closet box. They don't fit me anymore, but Dolores and Elenita are smaller and definitely thinner so the dresses will do — at least until we can do laundry. Mom even dug up some denim pants and a T-shirt I wore as a little kid. My mom never throws anything away, and that turns into a good thing. I hold up the pants and tee. Dolores nods and smiles. They'll fit César.

After baths and final cookies, everyone settles in for the night, and we begin our life as a newly formed family. We're not sure what tomorrow will bring, but for now everyone is safe and sound, or as safe as we can make them. Quickly I drift off next to GramZees. It's been a long day.

The screams jolt me awake. I hear Elenita's sobs and Dolores's soft whispers. "Está bien, Elenita, está bien." I don't know what Dolores is saying to Elenita, but the younger girl's cries turn to whimpers and finally quiet. I consider knocking on their door but decide not to. Dolores has dispelled whatever caused Elenita's nighttime terror. I lie awake in the dark for a long time afterward while GramZees snores softly beside me in the bed. Nothing disturbs her sleep. Sometimes it's an advantage to be a little hard of hearing.

My mind wanders through the events of the past days. We have taken on a lot all at once. I feel good that we have our guests out of the leaky shed, but I am a little scared about what could happen if our secret gets out. *Helping them is the right thing to do,* is my last thought as I drift back to sleep.

When I open my eyes again, GramZees has already slipped from the bed without my notice. I must have slept deeply even with the middle-of-the-night wake-up. It's still early, but I wander down to the kitchen and find my mom and grandma at the table drinking coffee. They are discussing "our situation." It's a code phrase we've agreed to use as shorthand for the secrets we are now hiding. "Loose lips sink ships," GramZees argued last night when we discussed the code. She remembers the warning from WWII when people feared enemy spies could overhear conversations. "Can't be too careful," she advised. Daddy chuckled that maybe GramZees was "a little over the top" with her cautiousness, but in the end we all agreed. So, "our situation" it is, and Mom and GramZees are discussing it.

"For everyone's sake, we need to find the grandmother as quickly as we can," GramZees says just as I walk into the room. "That's where the kids were headed and that's where they should be. Dolores is sure their abuela lives up in Melard."

"What happened to their parents?" Mom returns to the basic question. "How on earth did they all get separated and the kids end up on a train by themselves?"

"Still don't know," GramZees says. "I want to get their full story today if we can."

"Buenos días. Good morning," Dolores greets us. We didn't hear our guests come downstairs.

"Buenos días. Good morning," GramZees also uses both Spanish and English. Mom and I follow her lead. It's fun to be bilingual when I can pull it off. Mom motions for Dolores, Elenita, and César to sit with us at the table.

"¿Jugo de naranja?" I ask as I hold up a bottle of orange juice. Everyone nods yes.

"Coffee?" Mom holds up her cup as kind of a joke, but Dolores surprises her.

"¡Sí, café!" She's excited. Mom hesitates, but GramZees nods her head yes.

"The older kids in the migrant camps drink coffee all the time," she says to Mom, then turns to reassure Dolores, who looks confused by Mom's hesitation. "It's okay. Está bien. Está bien."

Mom sets a steaming cup in front of Dolores along with the creamer and sugar bowl. "Está bien," she repeats what GramZees said.

Está bien. Those are the same words Dolores said to Elenita to push away her screams in the night. "It's okay,"

Dolores soothed Elenita, "it's okay." But what? What's okay? What frightened her? I want to ask Dolores about it if I can figure out how. I have so much I want to find out, and I am frustrated not to speak the same language.

Despite the "situation" at our house, we still have canning to do after breakfast is done. Last night before dark, Daddy and I hauled in more green beans that have to be put up today. It's going to be a big job. We rarely have so many beans in one picking. After the breakfast dishes are done, Mom and GramZees organize the kitchen for the day's project. First, we need to wash the beans, then strip out the strings and snap the pods into bite-sized pieces. Mom will take them from there and finish the process.

Dolores and Elenita are eager to pitch in, so Mom puts us kids to work on the stringing and snapping part. GramZees washes the beans and picks through them to get rid of the ones with too many bug holes. César helps string and snap for a while, but his hands and attention wear out after a couple of batches. I find him some paper and a box of crayons. I have a Crayola 48-crayon set with every color you can think of and some shades the crayon people made up.

I'm not exactly sure what the girls say when I flip open the box top, but I can tell they like the colors. César is thrilled and ready to get to the coloring, so I set him up at the dining room table. He drifts back and forth to the kitchen to show us his pictures. Rainbows are a major theme.

Whenever he comes and goes with his multicolored creations, Elenita's eyes trail longingly after him. Dolores notices and finally says, "¿Quieres pintar también?" Elenita's eyes sparkle. I figure out that Dolores asked her if she wanted to color too.

"¡Sí! ¡Sí!" Elenita bobs her head, and then she is gone. Only Dolores and I are left in the kitchen. GramZees has finished her washing and sorting job, and Mom has a canner full and already steaming. They are taking a quick break while Dolores and I finish up with the stringing and snapping for the next batch.

"I heard Elenita last night," I start. Dolores looks thoughtful. Maybe she's trying to figure out what I said. I try again with some of the Spanish words I've learned. "La noche. Elenita. Cry." I don't know the word for cry, so I act it out while I say it. Then I remember how to ask why. "¿Por qué?"

Dolores understands. "Pesadilla. Bad dream," she says. "Un hombre malo en el tren. Bad man on train," she translates. I can see she wants to say more and is trying to find the English words so I will understand. "He tried to hurt us. When train stop, we run. Find little house." She points to the shed.

I am so frustrated that I don't speak Spanish! I can see there's a lot Dolores wants to tell me, and I want to hear it all. Maybe GramZees can help. I go into the front room to get her.

CHAPTER 15

"**S**he says her family was in Texas working on a big farm picking berries like every year," GramZees translates. The beans are forgotten, and Mom, GramZees, and I are huddled with Dolores around the kitchen table. "But after la Migra started the raids," GramZees continues, "they worried they'd get picked up and deported. Their parents were especially afraid that the family could be separated and the kids put someplace where they couldn't find them.

"It's shameful! Separating these families!" GramZees breaks from translation and throws out her own frustration in helpless outrage.

Dolores speaks in rapid-fire Spanish. "Mi abuela dice que la Migra no está molestando a los mexicanos acá en Ohio. Mis papás pensaron que estaríamos a salvo con ella."

"She says her grandmother told them la Migra is not bothering Mexicans where she lives. Her parents thought they would be safe there, in Ohio," GramZees clarifies, translating. Then she adds, "I've heard there are a lot of Mexicans who live in Melard year 'round and work the fields."

"How did your family get separated—split apart?" I ask, and I do hand motions so Dolores will understand my question.

"Es una larga historia." Dolores slowly shakes her head. I know it's going to be a long story.

"Papá nos llevó a donde se para el tren a llenarse de agua. Nos escondimos entre los montes hasta que se fuera la policía, y luego subimos a un vagón. Lo llamamos el tren de la abuela." Dolores pauses at the last memory.

GramZees is already interpreting. "She says her Papá took them to the place where the train stops to get water. They hid in the bushes to make sure the police were gone..."

"La policía look for mexicanos who hop the train." Dolores breaks into English to explain. She makes a hopping motion with her fingers.

GramZees waits to see if there is more, and then continues, "They climbed into a boxcar." GramZees pauses to smile. "They called it grandma's train. 'El tren de la abuela.'"

We sit for the next hour listening and asking questions as Dolores spills out the account of their journey. She tells us the boxcar bumped and rattled on for days—she doesn't know how many. Other Mexicans hopped on and off the car along the way. They were all going north where they heard it was safer. Everyone was very afraid. Her Papá didn't know exactly where the train was going, but the sun told him they were headed northeast, which was the general direction they needed to go to get to Ohio.

The family brought some food and water with them, but it wasn't enough for such a long trip. So, whenever the train stopped, Papá and some of the other men jumped off to get whatever they could find to eat and to share. One time their Papá almost didn't make it back in time. The train was already moving, and he had to run alongside to catch up. Another man pulled him back into the car. It was very scary, she tells us, and dangerous.

Finally, they arrived in Chicago. It was a big station, and the last stop for the other people in the car. They wished each other "Buena suerte — good luck" and said many sad goodbyes.

Because Dolores and her family were so close to Ohio, the run to safety seemed almost over. Soon they would be reunited with their grandmother, they thought, so they wanted to celebrate their journey. The Chicago station was full of people, and there were many places to buy food. Papá and Mamá decided to take a chance to get off the train together to bring back enough supplies for the little celebration and for the final leg of the trip.

The three kids stayed behind out of sight. At first, there was just the usual train station noise from outside. But then the shouting began. People were running along the tracks. Men were yelling in harsh-sounding English. Other terrified people screamed in Spanish, she tells us. She could hear doors bang open on the boxcars close by. Men shouted in bad Spanish, "¡Bájense! ¡Manos arriba! — Get out! Hands in the air!" La Migra was searching the cars one by one looking for Mexicans.

All the kids could do was wait and hope they would not be discovered. La Migra came — two men in uniforms with guns on their belts and flashlights in hand. Dolores says she was so scared she was sure they would hear her heart pounding. She was afraid that César might whimper and give them away, or that Elenita would cry out. But none of that happened.

"La Migra alumbró todo y luego se fueron — The border agents shined their bright lights around and then they left," Dolores tells us. The shouts and banging doors eventually stopped. The raid ended, and the kids waited for their mom and dad to come back. But they never came. After a while, the train lurched out of the station without their parents.

"We do not know what happened." Tears drip down Dolores's cheeks. "Papá and Mamá disappeared." César and Elenita come in from the dining room. They have been listening, and they are crying too. Mom waves them in. We circle around the three in a group hug.

"Está bien. Está bien," I whisper. And I so want it to be okay.

"We've talked enough for today," GramZees says. The kids have had all the remembering they can take for now. I know GramZees is right, but I still wonder about the bad man on the train who made nightmares for Elenita.

CHAPTER 16

A fter a quick lunch, Dolores takes Elenita and César upstairs for a rest. Mom, GramZees, and I settle in to finish the beans. "What a story," GramZees says. "What a terrible story."

"Breaks your heart," Mom adds. "No child should ever lose their parents like that. And no parents should every lose their children. Families are meant to stay together."

"Will they ever find each other? Will Dolores and Elenita and César ever see their mom and dad again?" I want to know.

"Hard to say," GramZees says. "Their parents were probably caught in the Migra raid that the kids escaped. I heard that they're targeting Mexicans in Chicago now too. Jailing and deporting them just like in Texas and California. Lots of migrants go to Chicago to work the farm fields and the slaughterhouses. La Migra will have easy pickings. It shames our country to treat decent folks this way."

"But will the kids ever find their parents?" I repeat my question.

"Some families I know in California are still looking, and it's been weeks since they got separated," she says simply. "Border Patrol doesn't always keep track of who they pick up or where they put them. People are there in the morning taking care of their family before work, and then gone by suppertime — disappeared, like Dolores says. The kids are left to fend for themselves. Some end up staying with relatives — aunts, uncles, cousins and such. But the relatives might get deported too. Some 'separated' kids get put in detention while la Migra tries to figure out what to do with them. Eventually they may get turned over to folks they don't even know. Kids end up getting hurt in a whole bunch of ugly ways. It's a sorry mess."

"We gotta find their grandmother," I say, stating the obvious. "And fast."

"For sure," GramZees agrees, "but how? That's the question. We don't even know their abuela's name." She smiles. "Probably won't work to go to Melard and start asking if anyone knows where grandma lives."

"Oh, GramZees, Dolores will know her grandma's real name." GramZees is only kidding, and we all need to laugh a little after the story we have just heard.

"'Course she will, but that still doesn't solve the problem." She ponders things. "It's the Mexican folks in Melard who will know how to find the grandma, but they'll be cautious of white folks snooping around. And I don't blame them."

"What about your California friends? Could they help?" Mom wants to know.

"Maybe," GramZees says slowly, "I'll give it a try. I got some numbers I can call. Maybe they will know some Mexican families in Melard who would be willing to talk to us." We have to leave it there for now.

But then I wonder if Daddy has union friends in Melard who know Mexican workers. "A long shot," GramZees says, "but we gotta try. We'll talk to your daddy when he gets home."

But Daddy just shakes his head no when we ask at suppertime. "I wish I could help, but not much union organizing going on in that part of the state. There oughta be, but there's not. Somebody should be organizing those farm workers into a union. They sure need one to get what's fair."

Seems like we are back where we started. We have finished supper and we're sitting around the table brainstorming. We need to find the grandma, and we have no one to help us. The only thing we know that's new is her name: María González Morales. Dolores says she's sure that's it, but GramZees mentions that may not be the name she uses in Melard. Migrants have to take fake names sometimes to stay hidden, she says. It's part of living in the shadows. Dolores nods in agreement. So, even knowing the grandma's real name may be another dead end. We sit in gloomy silence.

"Hey, Blue! Blue! You in there?" The voice through the screen makes us all jump. It's Jimmy standing on the front porch hollering through the open door. Dolores, Elenita, and César look around frantically for a place to hide. Mom, GramZees, and I freeze. Daddy too. We should've had a plan. Jimmy shows up regularly at suppertime, and we always invite him in for dessert. Normally, he'll yell through the door and I'll yell, "Come on in." But not tonight, not as long as we have our situation. Quickly, I grab a handful of chocolate chip cookies from the plate and sprint for the front door.

"Hey yourself, Jimmy." He's surprised by my abrupt appearance. I barely open the screen door and squeeze through the narrow sliver I make. "Want some GramZees goodies?" I shove the cookies toward him. I hope it will be enough to divert his attention from not getting his usual come-on-in welcome. He has eyes only for the sweets and seems to quickly forget that I didn't invite him inside. "Wanna ride bikes over to the new house on Cemetery?" It's the only thing I can think of on the spot. I desperately want to get him away from the house.

"Nah." He talks through a mouthful of chocolate chips and nuts. It's not pretty. *Why do boys do that?* I wonder. "Nah, the house is almost finished, and it's not interesting anymore." He's on his second cookie, and crumbs are spewing everywhere. I step out of the way. "Besides, my bike's got a flat." He finishes and starts on cookie number three. "There's a new *Gunsmoke* on in a few minutes. Let's listen to it instead. It's a brand-new episode." He's ready for cookie four.

"Not tonight," I say quickly. Our radio is in the front room. "Uh...uh...Mom's got a show she wants to hear." I hope he doesn't ask what the show is, but he does. "Oh, nothing you'd like." I step from the porch. "C'mon, let's go flatten some pennies."

Jimmy follows me down the steps to the backyard, but he grumbles all the way. "Don't see why we can't go inside and try your mom's show..." I just keep on walking toward the railroad tracks.

We stay on the tracks until dark when Jimmy's dad hollers him in for the night. I watch his shadow cut through our garden and across the Gallons' backyard, but I wait for his back door to slam before I head to the house. I don't want to risk him showing up at our door again tonight.

When I come inside, the house is quiet. Mom and Daddy are talking about going to bed early, and GramZees is moving in that direction too. Everyone's worn out. Our guests are nowhere to be seen. Jimmy's startling appearance has spooked them into hiding. I'm too wound up to be sleepy. For a moment I consider dialing channel ten to get the *I Love Lucy Show*, but instead find a seat in the back-porch swing. The night settles in around me. Even the moon is dark. Cicadas trill intermittently from somewhere in the yard, and crickets chirp from the flower bed by the stoop. Even Roscoe is tamed and purring contentedly on the chair cushion. Summer nights can soothe the soul, Mom often says, and I can use some soothing. I drift along in the gentle rocking of the swing. I'm almost asleep.

"Blue? Blue?" My name seems like a dream floating in air. "Blue? Blue?" The soft voice again.

"Dolores?" I whisper into the darkness. "¿Estás bien?" I'm pretty sure I asked her "Are you okay?"

"Sí. Estoy bien," she assures me softly. I breathe relief. She moves through the kitchen door like a ghost and takes a seat beside me. We gently rock back and forth in the old wicker swing. Two new friends who want to talk but are not sure of the words. Finally, Dolores speaks from the dark.

"We run from bad man." I know she means the man on the train. I wait for more. "He tried to touch me bad. Elenita too. Train stop for water. We jump, an' we run."

My mind flashes back to last summer and a dark movie theater in Roanoke, Virginia. My cousin, Georgia Anne, and I had gone to the picture show to pass the time while the grown-ups sat around in Aunt Elizabeth's kitchen to talk about whatever grown-ups talk about. Georgia Anne and I got popcorn and settled into center-section seats. We had the whole middle row to ourselves and a perfect view. About halfway through the show, I noticed a man sit down about five seats over. He kept glancing over at us. Georgia Anne was so into the movie, she didn't notice, but I kept my eye on him. Something wasn't right. After a few minutes, he moved two seats closer and was full-on staring at us. I couldn't see his hands. He had them between his legs. He fidgeted. I figured he was going to change seats again, so I punched Georgia Anne. "We gotta leave," I whispered, "right now."

"What?" Georgia Anne was confused. "In a minute. It's just getting to the good part."

"No! Now!" I got up and climbed over her to get her moving. We were halfway up the aisle when I glanced back at the man. He had vanished.

All this comes back in an instant, and I know with certainty why Dolores took her sister and brother and ran from their boxcar hideout into our shed. "Good to run." I reach for her hand in the dark. "He was bad, bad man." I let her know I understand.

"Sí," she responds. "No Papá. No Mamá. No help." I can hear tears in her voice, and I can hear how scared she was and is. Her family fled Texas to keep them all together, but their worst fear happened in Chicago anyway. Now the kids are easy prey for anyone who wants to hurt them. GramZees is right. Separating families is shameful and just wrong.

"Lo siento mucho, Dolores," I whisper into the darkness. It's not enough, not nearly enough to take away my new friend's fear, or confusion, or deep sadness for what has happened to her family, but "I am so sorry" is the best I know to say in Spanish. I put my arm around her, and we sit in silence while the swing rocks us. I can feel her sobs, but she makes no sound.

CHAPTER 17

om and GramZees are grim when I share with them what Dolores has told me. We are sitting at the kitchen table waiting for the coffee to perk. Daddy left for work an hour ago, and our other family has not come downstairs yet. "Those poor children," Mom finally says.

"Dolores is hardly a child anymore," GramZees says. "She's had to become both Mamá and Papá for Elenita and César." She shakes her head sadly. "She's done a fine job, no doubt, and her parents would be proud of her. They've raised her into a fine human being, but this is too much for any person her age to shoulder alone. We have got to get her some help—and fast." GramZees is back to finding the grandmother and reuniting at least some of the family.

"Talked to my California friends last night," she tells us as she spoons sugar into her mug, "but nothing there.

They don't know any Mexican families in the Melard part of Ohio." GramZees reaches for the creamer while Mom pours coffee into all three mugs — guess I'm old enough for coffee now. "But," GramZees says after her first sip, "they did suggest we contact some of the churches in Melard. They might know folks in the migrant camps."

I jerk my head up and smack my forehead. Some coffee sloshes from my cup onto the table. Mom and GramZees are startled. "Of course!" I say, "Rev. Adams! We've got to talk to Rev. Adams! If anyone knows church people in Melard who might help, he will." By the time Dolores smells the coffee and comes down to join us, we have a new plan ready to share.

We're finishing a second mug of caffeine and discussing my idea when Jimmy comes banging at the back screen door. He never shows up this early. We all freeze. Fortunately, the air is a tad chilly, and we haven't opened the kitchen door to the porch. If we had, Jimmy would easily see us — all of us — at the table. "Blue! Blue!" he yells through the screen. I hear the door rattle as he tries to open the screen, but it is still hooked — another lucky break.

"What are you doing here so early?" I startle him from behind. As soon as I heard Jimmy at the screen, I slipped out the front door and circled the house to the back. Jimmy whirls around to face me in the yard. He's too surprised to speak. "C'mon. I got tomatoes to pick." I start walking away from the house, and he falls in beside me. I think I have outsmarted him.

"What's going on, Blue?" He stops halfway to the garden.

"Wha'd'ya mean?" I try to sound nonchalant.

"You're not picking tomatoes. Where's your bucket?"

Oooops. He's a better detective than I gave him credit for.

"You're trying to keep me out of your house?" he says simply. He's on to me.

"Nah, GramZees is just not feeling well. That's all."

"I saw her yesterday. Looked fine to me," he counters. He's not going to let it go.

"Stomach started actin' up in the night," I say, but I know it's lame.

"Okay, Blue, maybe you got your reasons," Jimmy looks directly at me, "but I know you're not telling me straight. If I did something to make you mad, I'm sorry. I'll leave it at that so maybe we can get back to being friends." His words cut deep.

"Nah, it's nothing like that, Jimmy. We're still friends," I try to reassure him. "It's just that...well...we have a...a situation," I decide to use our family code word, "...and I just can't say anything more right now. So please don't ask me about it." I level with him as much as I can and hope he'll accept it.

"Ooo...kaaay..." is all he says as he nods his head slowly and stretches out the letters. He's got questions, lots of 'em, but he's doing his best to let them go, at least for now. I relax a little, but the whole thing has left me rattled.

It rattles Mom and GramZees even more when I tell them that Jimmy's suspicious. "This puts the rush on things," GramZees says. I can tell she's worried. "Get cleaned up, Blue, we're goin' to see the preacher."

"Well, that's quite a story," Rev. Adams says soberly after we share the situation from the beginning. We end with Jimmy's suspicions. "Quite a story," he says again. The three of us are seated in a circle of comfortable chairs in Rev. Adams's office at the church, and GramZees and I have been talking since we arrived. Rev. Adams broke in with a few questions along the way, but mostly, he's just let us tell our story.

"Well, here's some good news," he says, smiling at GramZees and me. "I have a great contact at the Methodist church in Melard."

"That *is* good news." GramZees's voice is relieved.

Rev. Adams says, "The pastor up there helps at the migrant camps—like you and your friends in California." He nods toward GramZees. "He's doing some of the same things as the church in Texas where we sent our carwash money." He looks at me. "Pastor's name in Melard is Dave Sagal—we went to seminary together. I'll give him a call today. It may take a little time, but I'm pretty confident he'll be able to locate the kids' grandma—if she's still there," he adds.

"But finding the grandma may be the easy part," he goes on. We look up in surprise. "The harder part is figuring out how to keep these kids safe until we do."

"We've got a real nice place for them at our house," I quickly put in, "and Mom and Daddy are totally okay with them hiding there, at least for now." GramZees nods in agreement. "And I can handle Jimmy," I throw in at the end, though I haven't figured out yet exactly how I am going to keep him away.

"I know," the preacher nods, "but those Mexicans are 'criminals,' you know that, don't you? And all your neighbors know it too." Our heads fly up. "Yep, the president said so on TV, so it must be true," he finishes sarcastically.

GramZees nods knowingly. "Yep, that's how it works, doesn't it?" She picks up on the preacher's point. "Ike says we have an invasion of bad people, and after a while, ordinary people believe it's true, even if it's not. Neighbors can turn against neighbors real quick."

"You are taking a big risk having the kids there," Rev. Adams's voice turns serious, "and the longer it goes on, the riskier it gets."

Jimmy pops to my mind again.

"We know we could go to jail," my grandmother says softly. "We don't want that, and we think it's wrong, but we just want to do what's right for the kids and their family."

Rev. Adams nods. He's still thinking. "But consider this: if the Border Patrol raids your house, they *might* arrest you," he speaks carefully, "but *for sure* they will take the Mexican kids. And when they do, the three of them will end up somewhere we don't know. They will 'disappear' just like their mom and dad. We won't be able to find them, let alone help them."

The danger for Dolores, Elenita, and César is suddenly more real. Keeping them safe at our house is more complicated than we have considered. Our family thought a lot about the risk to us if we took them in, but not nearly enough about the risk it poses for them. If Jimmy so easily grew suspicious, others could too. And they might be less friendly and more determined to uncover our secret.

The three of us sit in silence for a long moment. "Well, we're sure not gonna stick 'em back in the shed." GramZees clearly means to lighten things up. "Or send them on their way in a boxcar. Guess we'll just have to be extra careful," she says, becoming serious again, "and hope we can find their grandma really fast."

"That's the best we can do for now, I guess," Rev. Adams agrees. "I do have another idea, though, but I want to find out more before I suggest it. In the meantime, I'll call Dave Sagal to get things started in Melard." We are about to leave it at that when Rev. Adams adds, "I'd sure like to meet these kids."

"I'm sure that can be arranged." GramZees smiles.

CHAPTER 18

The Cs and I agree to meet up under the shady elm by the church. We chat about Willie's flavor-of-the-month ice cream — Peach Paradise — as we wait for Rev. Adams to finish a telephone call. We are headed to Mudsock for our weekly visit. Thanks to Connie's and my suggestion, Carla's now a regular part of the Mudsock team. When the preacher's call is done, we all load the trunk with groceries and head out for the delivery. The food isn't for the Harlan family anymore since Ted got a good job at the GM plant. But the Cs and I still like to hang out with Alice every week.

When we arrive in Mudsock, Rev. Adams parks the car in our regular spot, grabs several sacks of canned goods from the trunk, and walks toward a house two doors down. The Cs and I top the steps to the Harlans' front door just as Alice throws it wide open. "I baked us some cookies bigger 'an our heads!" she giggles.

We eat the "bigger-than-our-heads" sweets right off, then stay at the table to talk. Our voices are low because little Teddy's down for a nap, and Edith's asleep on Connie's lap. "You gotta finish school if you ever want to amount to anything," Alice says. We're discussing "life," as Carla calls our conversations. Life, and our futures. "I've always wanted to be a nurse," Alice shares. Connie nods. That's what she wants to be too, and she says so.

"Maybe we could go to the same nursing school," Connie says, beaming.

"That'd be real good." Alice smiles back. "But I gotta get my high school diploma before I can start."

"So do I," Connie reminds her. But we all know how much harder it's going to be for Alice because she had to quit school before she could finish.

"The preacher's trying to help me," Alice goes on. "He's getting me a tutor so I can get caught up and take the high school test."

"We could help you," Carla jumps in. "Maybe we could quiz you and stuff. Or at least we could babysit while you study." Connie and I agree.

Alice doesn't answer right away. "That'd be real nice," she says softly, after a minute. "Real nice." Connie takes charge. She pulls out her little calendar, and by the time the preacher arrives to pick us up, we have a babysitting schedule set up.

We make the short trip back to town, and Rev. Adams lets us off in front of Willie's so we can give Peach Paradise a try. We're still at the soda fountain counter licking the last sticky drips from our fingers. "We ought to have a slumber party," Connie announces from nowhere, "and invite the whole MYF." My friend takes her president's job seriously. "The Cedar Point trip's still a long way off, and we need something to stir things up. Summer's getting kinda boring."

For you, maybe, I think. *But it's sure not boring at our house! Any day we might all get arrested and sent off to jail!* That's what I want to say, but instead I add my "What a great idea!" to Connie's proposal. And it is, under normal circumstances, but my circumstances are off kilter at the moment.

"Yeah, great idea, but who's got a house that's big enough?" Carla's ready for specifics. "There's fifteen of us if everyone comes. And who wouldn't want a chance to stay up all night to eat junk and drink Coca-Cola with no parents around to stop you?"

"Oh, there'll be parents," Connie says glumly. "You think my mom's going let me go 'unchaperoned'?" She uses air quotes.

"Yeah, I know," Carla agrees. "But it was fun to think about for a second, wasn't it?" She grins. "Back to the real question. Where can we have this thing?"

"What about the church basement?" I blurt out. The idea popped into my head, and it seems like a good one. "It's big enough, and it's got the divider down the middle to make two rooms — one for the girls and one for the boys."

"Divider?! Well, you're no fun," Carla harrumphs.

"Just being practical." I shrug. "The 'chaperones' are going to be eagle-eyeing us anyway. You just want a chance to be alone with Bob Fox," I tease. "K-I-S-S-I-N-G in a tree." Carla turns pink but doesn't deny it.

"Okay. Okay. Stay on topic." President Connie's back on the job. "The church basement might work if we can get Rev. Adams to agree to it." That's all we need to hear. We leave Willie's in a rush and high-tail it to the church. Rev. Adams is surprised to see us again so soon, but he says he has a few minutes. It takes a lot of fast talking from the Cs and me, but the preacher finally agrees to the church slumber party. We'll present the idea to the MYF group on Sunday.

The slumber party talk has been a nice diversion, but on the walk home, my mind returns to my family's "situation." So far, Rev. Adams's preacher friend in Melard has come up empty. And in the meantime, Jimmy has gotten more and more curious. He shows up at our door at odd hours several times a day. He hopes he'll catch us at something, Mom thinks. It keeps us all on edge. Dolores, Elenita, and César have to be on constant alert to stay hidden from view. In some ways, life for them is not much better than being back in the shed.

On Sunday, Connie presents her idea for an all-nighter at the church, and it's a big hit with the MYF kids. Almost everyone signs up to bring snacks. There are loud groans when Connie mentions the part about chaperones, but Dale and Beth think their parents might be willing and promise to ask. Connie says her mother has already said yes. Everyone likes Mrs. Conklin, and she makes THE best chocolate sheet cake. The chaperone requirement has its upside.

Rev. Adams pulls me aside at the end of the meeting after the other kids have trickled away. "I'd like to come by your house tomorrow morning, Blue," he says in a low voice, "if that would be okay. I have some news on our situation." Rev. Adams is being careful too.

I try to read his face. Is his news good or bad? But I just say, "Sure. We'll be home all morning." I joke, "You can help us can tomatoes."

So, Rev. Adams comes around ten after we are long done with breakfast and deep into tomato peels...again. We have twelve quarts already lined up on the counter to cool and seal. The kitchen is even hotter and more steamy than usual because Mom has taken to closing the door to the porch in case Jimmy comes sneaking around.

We are ready to take a break when Rev. Adams announces himself at the back-porch screen door. GramZees has just put on a fresh pot of coffee, and Dolores and I are making lemonade. "Why don't we sit in the front room, Reverend." Mom leads the way out of the kitchen. "It's blazing hot in here. Blue, would you and Dolores carry in the lemonade?" she calls behind her. "And I think we've got some cookies in the jar. Bring them too."

Before she went to the door to greet Rev. Adams, Mom took off her apron and smoothed down her hair. She is a little nervous about having "that preacher" here. But when Dolores and I come with our pitcher and glasses filled with ice cubes, "that preacher" is relaxed on the floor racing Matchbox cars with César. "¿Te gusta el color rojo, César?" The boy beams at Rev. Adams's question and nods shyly.

He likes the color red. We are surprised to hear Rev. Adams speak Spanish. He says he studied it in college — a very long time ago, he reminds us — and now he's very rusty. "I speak Spanish un poco — a little." He smiles and adds, "Un poquito." He holds his thumb and finger almost together to show a tiny amount.

We chitchat, sip lemonade, and nibble cookies until we finally settle in to hear the news he has come to share. "Maybe we have found your grandmother," he starts. Tears of relief spring into Dolores's eyes as she quickly passes the news to Elenita and César in Spanish.

"She is in hiding," Rev. Adams says cautiously, "and she's afraid to answer many questions about her past or her family's, so it's hard to be sure she's the right person."

"But, my land, it's her own grandchildren! Why wouldn't she want to come forward?" We are surprised by Mom's outburst.

"Yes, it seems like a simple thing to us," Rev. Adams says softly, "but for her it's a risk. She goes by a different name in Melard, and she is afraid if she reveals her true identity, she might put herself...and her grandchildren in jeopardy."

"How?" Mom persists.

"Border Patrol's sniffing around Melard. That's new." Rev. Adams looks at Mom. "It's got folks upset." He pauses to gather his thoughts. "And worse, it seems that now the Melard police are in cahoots with the Border Patrol, and they've started showing up in the fields with border agents. They demand to see the workers' papers and arrest folks who can't produce them. People are afraid. And, they are very suspicious. When Dave's friends started asking questions in the camps, it got back to the grandmother. Probably scared her. She's afraid it might be a trick that will get her and her whole family arrested. With all these surprise raids going on, folks don't know who they can trust, so the safest way is to not trust anyone."

"How can we let her know it's safe?" I ask.

"Hold on a minute," GramZees says, raising her hand. "We need to let Dolores know what we are saying." I look at Dolores. She's confused and concerned. She can tell something's not right, but her English is not strong enough to follow our conversation. We take a breather while GramZees fills in the basics. She ends with a question. "¿Cómo podemos convencer a Abuela que hable con nosotros?"

"What did you ask her?" I want to know.

"I asked how we can convince this woman to talk to us," GramZees says. We wait while Dolores considers her answer.

"I write a letter." Dolores is definite. "Elenita and César can draw," she adds, pointing to the crayons and paper on the table. "We send photo so Abuela can know we are okay." It's a good plan and it just might work.

The photo's the hardest part. If we use Mom's Kodak camera, Willie's Drug Store has to send the roll of film away to be developed. It could take a couple of weeks. And Mr. Willie sees the finished pictures before we do. He's a gossip and likely to spread the word around town about our Mexican guests.

We talk to Daddy about it when he gets home, and he has the perfect solution. "We'll take a Polaroid!" he says. "I've been looking for an excuse to buy one of those new cameras. They say it develops the photo on the spot."

It takes us just two days to get it all done. Dolores has her letter sealed in a pink envelope, and Elenita and César have colored several pictures. They show Mexican women at the river washing clothes and men with machetes in the fields. Children are running free. Elenita likes to draw dancers wearing long, bright-colored skirts. César has rainbows everywhere.

Rev. Adams comes for supper to taste some of Mom's famous meatloaf and mashed potatoes. He's also going to be the photographer. He stands at the end of the table to get a good angle on everyone, especially on Dolores, Elenita, and César who are seated together at the other end. Dolores holds her letter in front of her and Elenita and César display their drawings.

"¿Listos?" Rev. Adams asks if we are ready. He snaps the image with the new Polaroid, then hands the camera to Daddy. Daddy's been practicing and expertly pulls the photo paper from the camera.

"We have to wait a few minutes to see the picture." Daddy lays the paper from the camera on the table to "process," he says. "Reverend, why don't you take another shot while we wait?" Daddy hands the Polaroid back to Rev. Adams and we all pose again.

Turns out we don't need the second one. The first is perfect. Daddy peels off the paper to show a clear black and white picture with Dolores, Elenita, and César in the center and the rest of us around the edges. If this doesn't convince the woman to talk, nothing will. "I'll get the whole package together and in the mail to Dave Sagal first thing in the morning," Rev. Adams says between big bites of meatloaf. "And then we just need patience and hope." He glances toward Dolores.

"Sí, paciencia y esperanza," Dolores says softly. We settle in to wait for the folks in Melard to do their work...but unexpected events overtake us.

CHAPTER 19

I haven't seen Jimmy around for several days — which is surprising. I'm glad he's quit surveillance, but I wonder why he's stopped coming over at all. I knock on the Micks' door. Jimmy's mom comes to face me. "What do you want, Blue?" She's never a warm fuzzy person, but this is abrupt even for her.

"Just looking for Jimmy, that's all." I keep it short.

"He's not playing today," she says and turns away.

"Tell 'im I stopped by," I yell through the screen at her retreating back. She just throws up her hand to say good-bye or maybe wave me away.

"Okay, then," I say to myself as I step off the porch, "I tried." When I get to the front sidewalk, I glance back and find Jimmy watching me from his bedroom window over the porch. He lifts his hand. I raise mine in return.

I tell GramZees about Jimmy, and she is as mystified as I am. "Just wait and see what happens," she says, shrugging. "Maybe he'll come around."

"Seems like we're just waiting and seeing about a lot of things these days," I say.

"And hoping for the best. Always hoping for the best."

It's two days before I hear anything else from Jimmy. It's almost dark, and I'm just coming back from the garden to put the hoe in the garage. "Blue! Blue! Over here," Jimmy's hoarse whisper startles me. He steps out from behind the lilac bush.

"Geeze, Jimmy, you scared me. What are you doing sneaking around in the dark?" I'm irritated, and it shows.

"Shhhhh! Keep your voice down, Blue. They'd kill me if they knew I was over here."

"Who'd kill you?" I lower my voice to match his.

"My mom and dad. And especially my Uncle Ray."

"Why would they kill you, for heaven's sake?" I'm not taking him seriously.

"'Cause you got wetbacks living in your house," he whispers sharply. My heart freezes solid. Silence hangs in the shadow between us.

"That's an ugly word, Jimmy," is what I finally say. "Don't call my friends that hateful name, or anyone else either."

Jimmy hesitates. "That's what Uncle Ray calls them,"

he finally whispers. His voice sounds like his chin is down in his chest.

Then I put out the question I dread, but must ask: "How does your uncle know who is staying in our house?"

"I told him," he mumbles. "And my mom and dad too. I told them what I saw. I told them those...Mexicans were having supper with you."

"You spied on us?" It's all I can think to say.

"I was only tryin' to find out why you didn't want me around," he says miserably. "And when I did, I was mad at you for not telling me. I'm sorry, Blue. I just wanted to get you in trouble."

"Well, you have, Jimmy," I say, "and you've caused some really bad trouble for a lot of other people too."

"I know that now, Blue," he says, "but I didn't know it then. You've got to believe that." His voice is desperate. We've settled down into the damp grass with our backs against the garage wall. No one can see us unless they come looking. I want to hear the whole story.

"I knew you were hiding something," Jimmy starts, "because you kept making excuses about why I couldn't go inside your house. One night, I waited outside your kitchen window. I could hear talking but I didn't understand most of it, so I peeked in to see what was going on. That's when I saw those Mexican kids eatin' supper with you, big as life."

"Oh, Jimmy, how could you?" I am so angry that he spied on us that I'm tempted to get up and leave. But I need to know the rest of what he did. I fear his second

crime is worse than his first. "And then what did you do?"
I ask evenly.

"Nothing right away. But then Uncle Ray stopped by
the house. He started going on about the Negroes moving
to Shortstop, over on Cemetery Road. It's gonna ruin the
town, he says. No white people want to live next to 'em."
Jimmy pauses before he pushes forward.

"Uncle Ray says Ike should round up all the blacks
and send 'em back to where they came from just like he's
deportin' the dirty Mexicans. He says we gotta stop the
'Mud People' from invading us. That's what he believes,"
Jimmy finishes in a gush.

"Do you believe that?" I stop him with a question.

Jimmy's quiet, then says, "Tell you true, Blue, I don't
know what to believe."

"How much did you tell him?" I ask.

"Only what I saw — three Mexican kids in your house,"
he says, then adds, "and I told him you didn't want me to
know about them." He realizes that's the worst part.

"And what did he say?" I ask softly.

"He said that he and his friends would put a stop to
it." Jimmy's quiet. "That's why I came to tell you, Blue. I'm
really sorry."

I believe he is, but that doesn't change things. We have
to act fast. La Migra might raid our house. Or maybe something worse could happen, if Uncle Ray and his friends
decide to "put a stop to it" on their own.

"How long ago did you tell your uncle?" I need the
details.

"Two days ago," he says.

I stand up and start walking toward the back door. "Thanks for warning us, Jimmy." There is no more time for talk.

CHAPTER 20

W e make a late-night call to Rev. Adams to tell him what's going on, and he comes over right away. "We've got to move the kids immediately," he says as soon as he walks in. "If you're on the target list, your house could be raided at any time. We have to get the children to a safer place." I have never seen him so serious or so agitated.

"But where?" Mom asks. "Seems like no place is really safe." She's upset too. We all are. Jimmy has put everyone at risk.

"They can stay at the parsonage tonight," Rev. Adams says. "I talked to my wife about it before I came over, and Jane's all for it. Our kids will love having guests." The parsonage is the house next door to the church where Rev. Adams and his family live.

GramZees is sitting close to Dolores to translate the parts of the conversation she doesn't get. When Dolores understands that they are moving tonight, she whispers the information to Elenita and César. They glance apprehensively at Rev. Adams. "Está bien," he gently tells them.

The preacher turns to me. "Blue, can you help them pack? We should get out of here, and quickly." Then, to my parents, "As long as the kids are here, they're in jeopardy and so are you. The sooner we leave, the better."

"But what about you and your family?" Daddy asks. "Won't you be putting them at risk?"

"We are okay for tonight, I think. They — whoever 'they' turn out to be — won't figure things out that fast. Tomorrow I have a new plan." This is new information. "I've been working on it for the last several days, but I didn't want to mention it until I was sure it would happen," he explains. "But these new developments have put the speed to it." We are all curious, but he says it's better we don't know until everything is in place.

Dolores and I head upstairs with the other kids to collect their few belongings. I give César and Elenita the big box of crayons to take with them and the Matchbox cars that Daddy bought for César. Dolores and Elenita carefully fold their clothes and place them in the small suitcase that Mom has loaned them.

When we come downstairs, the grown-ups are in serious conversation with a person we have not met. "Come join us." Rev. Adams waves us over. "This is Ms. Linsky. She's an attorney who knows a lot about immigration and the law. Dave Sagal put us in contact. She's here to help us."

Women can be lawyers?! It's the first I've considered it. I'm thrilled. I'll ask GramZees about it later. It's the kind of thing she will know about.

Ms. Linsky smiles at us all, then greets Dolores, Elenita, and César in soft, fluent Spanish. After that, she's all business. "Rev. Adams has briefed me on the situation," she starts. "I'm here to make sure you understand what your rights are and how to protect yourselves in this situation." She hands each of us a piece of paper that has English on one side and Spanish on the other. *KNOW YOUR RIGHTS! ¡CONOCE SUS DERECHOS!* is printed across the top in dark black letters.

Ms. Linsky says, "In the United States, we have constitutional rights that protect us even if we are not a citizen." She repeats this in Spanish, then returns to English. "If the police or la Migra show up at your house, do not let them in unless they have a warrant signed by a judge. They cannot come inside without your permission. That is your right." GramZees nods. She knows this from California.

"And you have the right to remain silent," Ms. Linsky continues. "Do not tell the officers anything! Even if it seems simple." She is very adamant about this. "You do not want to risk saying something that can be used against you or risk revealing information that can be used to find the kids." Mom and Daddy are taking all this in.

"And, Blue," GramZees says to me, "this is for you too. Don't give permission for any police of any kind to come into the house and don't tell them anything. Nothing."

Ms. Linsky nods agreement. "If anything like this does happen, tell the officers you want to consult your lawyer." She hands us each a business card with her name and telephone number. "Call me right away. I will come and help you."

When she is finished explaining in English, she repeats it all in Spanish. "It's pretty simple," she tells us English speakers. "Don't open the door. Remain silent. Ask for a lawyer. If they say they have a warrant, examine the paper very carefully to make sure it is signed by a judge. Sometimes la Migra tries to fool people with phony documents so they can get inside."

When Ms. Linsky is finished, we ask a few questions, then she leaves. Rev. Adams pulls his car close to the back door so Dolores, Elenita, and César can get in quickly. We do hugs all around before they go out. "Muchas gracias," Dolores says.

"We'll talk tomorrow," Rev. Adams says as he goes for the door. We four stand for a moment as the car's taillights fade away. The whirlwind events of the evening have thrown us all off balance.

"Five-thirty comes early," Daddy finally breaks into our thoughts. We know it's time for bed. It may be an eventful night.

CHAPTER 21

The night passes without anyone banging on our doors or burning a cross in our front yard—something white supremacists like Uncle Ray might do, Daddy says—but that does not keep us from being jumpy. I hear Daddy up sometime after midnight, then Mom, then Daddy again. During the night, I make several trips to the bathroom, and the light in GramZees's room never goes off. At first I wonder if she has fallen asleep with the lamp on, but I can hear rustling paper and decide she must be reading. I've just drifted off when I hear Daddy get up to go to work. I give up and go downstairs. Mom and GramZees are there too, sitting with Daddy at the kitchen table. All heads are deep into coffee mugs, and I pour a full cup for myself. I hope the Adams family and their guests had a better night than we have had.

We are back to waiting, but ten o'clock passes, and we still have not heard from the preacher. We are anxious to know if everything and everyone is all right. And we are super curious about the "new plan" Rev. Adams mentioned last night. "Well, I guess no news is good news," Mom says. "Or maybe not." She's been fidgeting all morning, flitting from one project to the next. GramZees has been keeping up with Mom in the fidget department. And, so have I. We won't relax until we hear something. We consider walking up to the parsonage to check but decide against it.

"Better not," GramZees says. "If anyone is watching the house, we don't want to lead them right to the kids." She is right to be cautious. So, we settle in to wait and wonder. Roscoe wanders in and demands buttermilk. I fill his bowl on automatic.

Finally, the phone rings and it's Jane Adams with a message. "John says to meet him at the church. He's there now waiting for you."

I don't think we have ever walked faster to cover the half-mile to the church. We arrive at the side door breathing heavy and ready to hear what the preacher has to say. We are surprised to find the door locked, but Rev. Adams opens at our first knock. "I figured you'd get here in a hurry," he says with a smile, his sharp blue eyes sparkling with humor. We relax. Whatever is coming will be okay.

"Follow me," he motions, "I've got something to show you." He is careful to lock the outside door behind him. We wind through the narrow hallway and up a flight of stairs to the classrooms where the church holds Bible study on Sundays before the "singin', prayin', and preachin'." I have never done any of this myself, but that's what Connie tells me happens on Sunday. We pass several little rooms on the way to the last door. Rev. Adams taps softly when we get there.

To our surprise, Dolores swings open the door. Elenita and César are standing beside her, and they all break out in big smiles when they see us. Dolores opens the door wider. "Bienvenidos a nuestra casa nueva," she says. Welcome to our new house. We look confused, because we are. We thought our friends were at the parsonage next door, but here they are at the church instead.

The classroom has had a makeover. There are made-up beds around the sides and a round table in the center covered with a flowered cloth. Stacks of plates and bowls line the bookshelves, a small refrigerator hums in the corner, and some simple groceries and fresh fruit sit on another shelf. It does look like a little house.

"This is the new plan," Rev. Adams begins to explain. "Shortstop Methodist is offering a safe place—a sanctuary—where César, Elenita, and Dolores can stay until they are reunited with their family."

"This *is* a new plan!" GramZees says, astonished.

Rev. Adams goes on. "I got the idea from my friends in Texas. They have a whole network of churches that house migrants hiding from the Border Patrol. So, I figured, why not? We could be the first church in Ohio to do that."

"How'd you do this all so fast?" GramZees means the little house setup.

"The simple answer is that there are some really good people at Shortstop Church," Rev. Adams says, beaming, "and they decided to open their hearts even when it's a risk." He takes a breath. "The longer answer is, we held an emergency meeting late last night. *Really* late." He smiles and yawns. "Ms. Linsky was there to help on the legal matters, but after the council heard the kids' story, they voted unanimously to open the church, at least for now. We want to get the whole congregation on board before we make it permanent. It's a big decision, and some people are not going to agree with it, but we are going forward. It's an emergency situation."

"But are Dolores, Elenita, and César safe here?" Mom wants to know. "Can't the Border Patrol come take them just like at our house?" I want to know that too. "Can't they do a raid at the church just like other places? And can't they arrest you like they could arrest us?"

"Yes, legally they can do all of those things," Rev. Adams speaks slowly, "but they probably won't." He reaches out to gently draw Dolores, Elenita, and César to him. "This family has asked for sanctuary inside Shortstop Church, and we have taken them in." Rev. Adams's voice has authority like he's talking to border agents banging on the church door. Maybe he's practicing what he will say if he has to.

"You think that's enough to stop them?" Mom is still worried.

"There's no law that the Border Patrol *has* to respect the church boundary, but it's rare for them not to. It's a risk, but it's worked other places and we are betting that it will

work here. It's the best chance we have of keeping everyone safe until we can reunite the family." There's a gentle
knock. "I think lunch has arrived," Rev. Adams says as he
reaches to open the door. A white-haired couple—some of
the "good people" the preacher mentioned, I guess—bring
in several covered dishes that leave a trail of good smells
behind them.

Before we head back home, we learn that Mr. and Mrs.
Taylor, the lunch team, have organized several families to
bring meals every day. "But we don't want folks just to drop
food off," Howard Taylor says. "We want them to sit down
and break bread so our church families and our sanctuary
family can get to know each other a little."

"Do you need more volunteers?" Mom surprises us.
"We can bring supper one night if you need us." So, it's
agreed that we will provide the meal every Friday.

The Taylors also are signing up volunteers to spend
the night at the church. "We need an adult around at all
times," Rev. Adams explains, "just in case." He means if
la Migra does show up or anyone else with bad intentions.
GramZees and I say we want to take a turn. I have no doubt
that GramZees could take on anyone who comes to the
door. I am beginning to believe I could too.

Martha Taylor mentions that she wants families with
children to visit Elenita and César. "I tell them to bring some
toys and games. Language doesn't matter so much to kids
playing. They always figure it out."

"I can call some MYF kids," I suggest. "I bet a lot of
them would come to meet Dolores." Rev. Adams agrees.

"Do we have to stay inside the church all the time?" I'm thinking about Peach Paradise at Willie's. Dolores loves ice cream and the drug store is just a two-minute walk away.

"The kids don't have to stay inside the church building," Rev. Adams says, "but they MUST stay on church property or they can be arrested. Ms. Linsky was very clear about this. The grassy areas around the church are okay as long as they don't go past the far edge of the sidewalk. We must be careful."

Dolores and Elenita nod. They clearly understand. César? Maybe. But he's only five.

"We can have an ice cream party on the front grass." I quickly adapt my idea. "It'll taste just as good."

CHAPTER 22

"How come you know so much about these Mexican kids?" Connie wants to know. She's suspicious, but Ms. Linsky advised us not to tell anyone we had hidden undocumented people at our house, even if they are not there now.

"The family's gone," Ms. Linsky explained, "but you did harbor them, and that's still illegal. Don't go spreading your story around, or you're admitting to a crime." So, I struggle to answer my friend's question and at the same time step around the forbidden topic.

The Cs and I are at the R & R having late-afternoon Coca-Colas. Three empty pretzel boxes litter the table, and we are into our second round of Cokes. I want them to go with me to the church to meet Dolores, but the invitation has turned into a big discussion—exactly what I hoped to avoid.

"I know them, because I've met them." I sound defiant. "And if you would just come with me, you'd get to know them too. I promised Rev. Adams I would get some MYF kids to visit. Don't you want to meet them?"

"Of course I do, that's not the point. The point is you're hiding something. I know it." Connie narrows her eyes at me. "And real friends don't keep secrets from each other. That's all I'm going to say."

"Okay, let's go." I decide to seize the moment before Connie starts her interrogation again. Carla has been mostly quiet, but as soon as I say "go," she stands. On the way to the church, I share the parts of Dolores's story that I can. I give the Cs the basics: The family is from Mexico and they worked in the fields picking crops in Texas. "They're like the migrant farm workers we saw in the slides Rev. Adams showed us," I say.

"Where are their parents?" Carla asks on the way. "And why are the kids staying at the church in...what do you call it?"

"Sanctuary," I say. "The church is providing a safe place for them until some of their family can be found. I don't know where the mom and dad are." Which is all true, but I don't say anything about the family running from la Migra in Texas, or the boxcar ride across the country, or the Operation Wetback raid in Chicago that "disappeared" the parents. And I don't mention the search for their grandmother in Melard. GramZees's "loose lips sink ships" motto is ringing in my ears.

"How can we talk to them?" Connie switches topics.

"We don't speak Spanish." She's getting a little nervous about the meet-up.

"Dolores speaks some English—enough to get us started," I reassure her. "It'll be a little awkward at first, but it'll be okay. You'll see."

And it is. As usual, Connie is a little-kid magnet. Not long after we get there, César is sitting beside her and they are "reading" a book together. Connie points to something in the picture, and César says the Spanish word. Then César points, and Connie says the word in English. Pretty soon, they expand the game to include objects around the room.

Elenita has her own ideas about fun, and she invites Carla to color with her. Dolores and I sit at the table with them and ooooh and ahhhh at each masterpiece. While she colors with Elenita, Carla relaxes enough to strike up a simple conversation with Dolores. "Where are you from?" she starts.

"I am from Mexico," Dolores replies.

"How old are you?" Carla speaks very slowly and a little too loud. She wants to be sure Dolores understands.

"You can just speak normally," I say quietly.

"I am..." Dolores starts, then looks to me for help. "¿Cómo se dice trece?"

"Thirteen," I say. I'm pleased that I can answer. The Spanish books from the bookmobile have helped, and Dolores is a patient teacher when we talk together, and GramZees too.

"I am thirteen years," Dolores answers Carla. "How old are you?"

"I am twelve."

"¿Doce?" Dolores looks at me.

"Sí," I nod. "Twelve."

"How do you say twelve?" Carla wants to know.

"Doce," Dolores answers. And so it goes for the rest of the afternoon until the supper team comes with food.

"We'll bring ice cream next time," Connie promises when we leave. All eyes sparkle. Everyone knows what that means. "Ice cream" doesn't require translation.

"That was really fun!" Carla says as soon as we hit the sidewalk. "I'm so glad you convinced us to come."

"Me too," Connie jumps in. "And, Blue, I'm sorry about before. I know you have your reasons for keeping the secret, whatever it is. I won't ask any more about it. Okay?" I nod.

———

After our visit, president Connie swings into action. Within days, she has things set up to get the MYF involved to welcome Dolores, Elenita, and César. She has invited "our Mexican friends," as she calls them, to be guests at our next meeting. And she asks Dolores to talk to the group about what life is like in Mexico. Dolores hesitates to say yes, but Rev. Adams encourages her, and GramZees says she will help translate and navigate around forbidden topics like "Where are your parents?"

The Sunday night plan is set, but Rev. Adams has a special request. "I know you are in charge of your MYF programs," he says, "but just this once, I would like to have a little time to talk during the meeting. I want to explain more about why our church is providing sanctuary for Dolores, Elenita, and César and what that means. The MYF has an important part to play."

"That would be great!" Connie is excited.

"And just so you know, this week's sermon is going to be about the same things." Rev. Adams smiles. "You could come Sunday morning and get a double dose." I know his teasing is meant for me.

But teasing or not, I take the challenge and roust myself out of bed early on Sunday to get to the church before the nine o'clock start time. Since I've never been to the preaching and praying part of church, I don't want to go it alone. The Cs have promised to meet me so we can go to the service together. Sundays start slow at our house, and I leave before Mom and Daddy come downstairs. I heard GramZees go out earlier on some mission of her own. She has her ways, Daddy always says.

I can hear the organ music about a block from church. It drifts out the open front doors and surrounds the dressed-up people who gather in small groups to chat on the sidewalk. My friends are there just as they promised. We greet each other as the tower bell bongs the signal for folks to go inside.

The Cs and I follow the other church-goers to find a seat, and I get my first taste of Sunday church. Colored-glass windows line the walls on both sides of the big room, and the sun that shines through gives everything a gauzy, multi-colored look. Up front under a spectacular window that goes all the way to the ceiling, there's a high table with two white candles and a brass cross set between them.

The last people rustle in and get settled in the pews. Action begins with a kid, about Elenita's age, who comes up the aisle holding a long brass stick. She heads to the front and uses the stick to light the candles on either side of the cross. This must be some kind of secret signal, because the organ blasts and everyone stands up to sing. Rev. Adams comes flowing up the aisle in a long black robe and takes his place in the front.

Things get busy after that with lots of getting up and sitting down, and a fair amount of singing, praying and regular talking in between. I keep my eye on the Cs so I know what I am supposed to do. At one point, four men pass around some baskets. I drop my quarter in the one that comes by me. Mom had told me this would happen, so I am prepared. Finally, Rev. Adams swishes his way to the speaker's spot.

I don't understand much of what the preacher says, but I snag on to a couple of things. He starts with the Bible: "Leviticus 19:34," he tells us. I have no idea what the Leviticus thing is about, but Rev. Adams reads it out loud, so it doesn't matter. "'You must treat the foreigners living among you as native-born and love them as yourself.'" There's more about somebody being in Egypt, but I didn't get that. I drift off.

I perk up later when Rev. Adams mentions Henry David Thoreau. Mrs. Shultz, our sixth-grade English teacher, was big on Thoreau. The preacher is too. "The great

thinker, Thoreau, believed ordinary people have an obligation to break the law," he starts.

Really? Mrs. Shultz never mentioned that. I'm listening.

"People have an obligation to break the law,"
Rev. Adams repeats Thoreau, "...*if the law is unjust,*" he
emphasizes.

Mmmm? Now I am *really* listening.

"*Breaking* the law may be the only way to get the law
changed." The preacher finishes with Thoreau.

The "breaking the law" thing is still knocking around
in my head when Rev. Adams spins off to talk about
Jesus. Turns out, Jesus was a law breaker, according to the
preacher, especially laws that hurt poor people. Of course,
all Jesus' law breaking made some important people mad,
and it got him killed in the end. Even I know that. So that's
something else to think about.

Rev. Adams says a lot more, but that's the best of it
that I can remember. All in all, I know he's explaining — in a
long-winded, roundabout way — why Shortstop Methodist
is helping Mexican kids who are running from la Migra.
Seems kinda like the thing Jesus would do; at least, that's
the way Rev. Adams sees it. And, doing like Jesus is pretty
important to churchy folks.

But here's a surprise: Somewhere in there, I get the feeling the preacher is talking directly to me. He's probably not
really, but it seems like it. My family may not be "churchy,"
but we did the right thing to help Dolores and the other kids.

Rev. Adams (finally!) finishes up. "Today, we welcome our sanctuary family to Shortstop Methodist Church.

Dolores, Elenita, César. Please come forward. Por favor, adelante." He waves them up the aisle. The organ throbs and everyone starts singing, "Bless be...eee the tie...ie that binds..."

And wouldn't you know it? GramZees is right behind Dolores, Elenita, and César coming up the aisle. She's going to translate. She never said a word to me ahead of time. She has her ways, as Daddy says.

———————————

"That was quite the welcome party," GramZees says on the way home. All the church hoop-la ended downstairs with cookies and punch, and the Cs and I stood right beside our Mexican friends and introduced them to folks who came to welcome them.

"What do you think about that Johnson guy?" I ask GramZees. After most people had cleared out of the church basement, a reporter for the *Central Ohio Star* showed up. Rev. Adams knew him and had agreed to let him do an article on Shortstop Methodist. By the time the talking was done, Dolores agreed to do an interview to tell their family's story, and GramZees said she would share about her work in the migrant camps out in California. And the Cs and I accepted the offer to be "the voices of young people" in Mr. Johnson's piece.

CHAPTER 23

r. Johnson works fast, and his article appears the following week in the *Central Ohio Star* Sunday edition. The piece takes over the front page and continues on to page A-2. It includes lots of photos, even one of GramZees reading a book with César and Elenita, and a group picture of the Cs and me with Dolores at the MYF meeting.

"Well, I see we have some people in our family who made the news," Daddy teases as we stand around the kitchen table with the Sunday paper spread open over the top. We've already read Mr. Johnson's article out loud two times.

"He did a good job," GramZees says, meaning the reporter. "I'm glad he included some meat."

"Meat?" I ask.

"Meat. Substance. Real news. He could have just stuck to the human interest part—three lost kids, local church folks trying to help, stuff like that. That's interesting, but the real story, the meat, is Ike's Operation Wetback policy." GramZees points to the article. "Johnson did his homework. The kids' story puts a human face on the ugly things happening in our country."

"He wrote a good piece," Mom agrees. "And I'm glad he never mentioned us or our shed." She smiles. She was worried, I guess, but I figured Ms. Linsky would keep us out of it. The lawyer agreed to review the piece before publication to make sure there was nothing that put anyone in legal jeopardy.

GramZees and I are going to church this morning, and when we arrive, people are all a-twitter. The usual dressed-up crowd stands on the sidewalk outside the main door waiting for the tower bell to ring, and everyone is talking about the front page spread in the *Star*. Several folks have brought copies of the paper just in case others haven't seen it, and people cluster in little groups looking at the photos.

As I search for some MYF kids to hang with, I notice six or seven scruffy-looking guys milling around across the street in front of the hardware store. I do a double take when I recognize one of them. It's Bobby Jack, the guy who threatened Rev. Adams on the TV news. He didn't have any use for the preacher, so what's he doing here on a Sunday morning? Did he have some kind of conversion? I watch them all closer to see if they cross over to the church. They don't. They just huddle a minute, then line up to stare over at us. A guy with a megaphone steps to the front and aims his mouthpiece in our direction.

"Hey, Churchies!" The sound blasts toward us, and our heads jerk to attention. "Hey! Over there! You deaf?" the man barks. "Listen up. We got a message for ya. Tell your wet-back-lovin' preacher that we don't want no Mexicans here!"

Megaphone Man turns to his gang. "Right? We don't want 'em here!"

"We don't want 'em here!" they shout and raise their fists in the air.

"You hear us?" Megaphone Man points his finger at us like a gun.

"We don't want 'em here!" the thug-pack barks support.

As if on cue, a rusty Chevy rolls from the alley. Six more men jump out to join the crowd. The newcomers hold signs printed in bold capital letters. Megaphone Man raises one high over his head for all to see.

He yells out the first line, "THE ONLY GOOD MEXICAN..."

"IS A DEAD MEXICAN!" the gang screams out the second line.

The megaphone blasts bring Rev. Adams to the door in his black preacher robe. He pauses on the church steps to take in the situation, then walks to the edge of the sidewalk directly across from the mob.

"Friends," the preacher raises his voice over the chants. "Friends." His words are strong and even. "Come join us. Our church is open to all who enter in peace. We welcome you."

Megaphone Man turns up the volume.

Rev. Adams repeats the invitation.

The "dead Mexican" chants get louder.

Rev. Adams turns back and ushers us into the church.

The megaphone and the thugs are gone by the time church is over. But the whole thing has left us unsettled. The preaching and praying went on like normal, but we could hear the hateful taunts from outside well into the morning. When we first filed into the building, Rev. Adams had a quick conversation with Mr. Taylor and five other men from the congregation. Four of them moved to the back and stationed themselves by the doors. The two others stepped outside to keep watch.

"Not surprised we got the 'crazies' on us," GramZees says on the way home after church. "But I am surprised at how fast they got organized. They must have been planning it already and the newspaper story got 'em extra riled. Looked like outsiders to me. You recognize any of 'em, Blue?"

"Maybe," I say slowly.

GramZees turns her head to me. "Who?"

"One was the guy I saw on TV who threatened Rev. Adams a while back," I say. "And...I think Jimmy's Uncle Ray was the guy with the megaphone," I finish in a rush.

"Oh, my land!" Even GramZees is shocked.

We share the news as soon as we get home, and Mom and Daddy are grim-faced. The disruption on the sidewalk was bad enough, but to learn that Jimmy's uncle was in the lead is a sobering turn. Uncle Ray and his gang might come after us, Daddy thinks. Mom is convinced that we'd be an easy target for their hate.

CHAPTER 24

I haven't seen Jimmy around since the night he confessed. Maybe he's avoiding me on purpose, I'm not sure, or it could be his parents have ordered him away. I don't know that either, but I do know I miss him. Summer is not the same without him. So, I am extra tickled when I spot him up on the railroad tracks behind our house after the Sunday uproar at church.

"Hey," I say from the corn stalks. He looks up. I don't think he's surprised. Maybe he wanted me to see him. "Wanna do pennies?" I say, like normal. Like old times. Like before all the window-peeking business and what came after.

"Sure." He flashes a hopeful grin.

Jimmy has a bag full of coins to get us going, and when we run out, I go fetch my cigar box from under the bed. We start with pennies, move to nickels, then dimes, and finally do a couple of quarters. At first, it's something familiar and comfortable to do. Something that keeps us from having to talk about the BIG stuff that hangs between us. But as the afternoon goes on, the shared fun opens some gentle breathing space between us that somehow makes it okay to talk. Really talk.

We are sitting in the grass by the tracks waiting for the next locomotive to steam past us, and Jimmy starts the conversation. "I saw your picture in the paper. It was interesting about the Mexican kids." I nod, but don't say anything. Then he says how sorry he is about the stuff he did. And I tell him I am sorry that I had to keep the secret that made him so angry at me. He says he understands it now.

We finally get around to talking about what happened Sunday and about my seeing his uncle leading the mob outside the church. He doesn't say anything for a long while, and I am afraid I've gone too far. But then he surprises me. "My uncle's wrong hitchin' up with that group," he says. "My dad and mom are trying to talk some sense into him. They told him he's just gonna get himself in trouble running with that crowd. They're up to no good, my dad says, but Uncle Ray's not listening. Says he doesn't want to hear it." Jimmy shrugs in resignation.

It's almost time to go in, and I'm working up to a question I've been wanting to ask since I first spotted him up on the tracks this afternoon. "You want to meet 'em?"

"Who?" he asks, but maybe he knows.

"The migrant kids," I say, "Dolores, Elenita, and

César." He's hesitant, I can see that. "They're living at the church," I say. "They're there to be safe, or at least we hope they're safe. But after yesterday, I'm not so sure. Anyway, do you want to meet them?"

"Let me think about it," he says finally. "I'll let you know tomorrow."

Jimmy is true to his word, and he knocks softly on our back door around ten in the morning. "Blue, you in there?" he calls through the screen.

"Come on in, Jimmy," Mom says. She sounds friendly and relaxed. Mom's not one to hold a grudge. "Blue's down getting a load of wet sheets out of the washer. Cookies in the jar if you want one. Milk's in the icebox like always." I hear the conversation from the basement, and I'm glad Mom's treating Jimmy like before. I top the stairs with the clothes basket.

"Don't get your hand stuck in there," I tease when Jimmy's fist comes up stuffed with GramZees's oat-meal-raisin deliciousness. He grins. Roscoe slides his silky side against Jimmy's leg. It's a cat welcome, not a demand. Roscoe has missed Jimmy too.

Jimmy brings the cookies outside and munches slowly through his stash while I pin wet sheets to the line. It's a perfect day to dry clothes and they'll be crisp in an hour, maybe less. "Gave it some thought," he says. "I want to meet the Mexican kids."

"Their names are Dolores, Elenita, and César," I say as I pin the last sheet to the line. "We can go this afternoon if you want."

"That'd be good," he says through cookie crumbs. "Can I hang out here till it's time? Nothin' fun to do at home."

I nod.

Jimmy and I play five-hundred rummy until lunch, and it's a close contest. But I eventually beat him out with a three-ace spread worth forty-five points. "That puts me over the top." I lay out the aces and toss my last queen to the discard pile. It's hard not to gloat a little, because Jimmy's a good player and almost always wins.

"Count 'em up," he says, not willing to concede. We re-add the score and I finally convince him.

"If I would've held on to that ace of hearts, you couldn't have gone down." He's still replaying the game later over peanut butter and jelly sandwiches.

"Woulda, coulda, shoulda," I tease, but I'm done with the card game. "You ready?" I put my plate in the sink. We hit the sidewalk and make for the church. Mr. Hill is sitting by the side door reading a book in his fold-up lawn chair. He rises to greet us. After the Sunday incident, the church council decided to station a watcher at the doors 24/7. The whole thing has put everyone at the church on alert.

"Hey, Blue. Hey, Jimmy. You two here on official business?" Mr. Hill tries to lighten the situation. "Must be important if you're here, Jimmy," he teases. The Micks are C and E Christians, Connie says, meaning they come to church only on Christmas and Easter.

"People got a right to make their own choices," GramZees said when I mentioned the C and E thing. Seems true to me. But I'm glad that Jimmy made the choice to come with me today.

"Here to visit our new family," I say. Mr. Hill nods and brings out his keys.

"Good timing," he says as he unlocks the door and opens it for us. "I think the kids are in the basement looking for something to do."

Dolores, Elenita, and César are where Mr. Hill said, and our timing *is* good. All three kids beam when they see us because our arrival has saved them from a boring afternoon. I do quick introductions and we get a game of Skittles started. Everyone is a little shy in the beginning, but things relax when the game gets going. Dolores has been practicing and she's getting pretty good—better than me, but not quite as good as Gary, the MYF Skittles champ. She almost beat him at the last meeting, but he edged her out in the last round.

Jimmy's pretty good at Skittles too, but he spends a lot of his time helping César wind his string on the spinner. He's very patient, and he figures out pretty fast that it's better to show rather than talk. "Like this," he says as he demonstrates. "Not this," he points and shakes his head. He means don't overlap the winds or the string will get tangled. With Jimmy's help, César gets better and better as the afternoon goes on, and when he knocks down six pins in one turn, Jimmy is as proud as the five-year-old.

"That's a good place to stop," I say and start cleaning up. "I told Mom I'd be home by five to help with supper."

César's face falls, but then it lights with a smile when Jimmy and I promise to come back tomorrow for a rematch.

"They're just like regular kids," Jimmy says as we walk back home.

"They *are* regular kids," I say. "Regular kids who have had a lot of bad things happen to them that should never have happened." Jimmy is quiet.

———————————

As promised, Jimmy and I show up at the church the next morning to hang out with Dolores, Elenita, and César. The Cs are there too, and since we have a good number, we decide to go upstairs to the classroom part of the church to play hide-and-seek. The rule is we can hide anywhere as long as we stay on the second floor. Carla is "it" and starts counting while the rest of us scatter to find good hiding places. Connie flattens herself behind the window curtains in a room facing Main.

"All-e-all-e-in-free!" It's Connie's voice that summons us, and we are surprised. We've just got ourselves hidden, and she's not "it." Carla is. But we come out anyway to see what's up. We gather at the window beside Connie. She's all serious. "Look at this." She points to the sidewalk below.

Jimmy's Uncle Ray is there, megaphone in hand to work a crowd of twenty or thirty scruffy men. He shakes hands and slaps backs till he's greeted everyone. I glance at Jimmy. His face is pale and intent. He and I are the only ones at the window who know the identity of Megaphone

Man. We all watch in dismay as the group below us grows larger and louder. "Don't these people have better things to do?" Carla wants to know. "It's the middle of the week. They should be at work."

I get home, and right away tell GramZees and Mom about the new developments. "When I saw 'em Sunday, I was afraid of this," GramZees says grimly. "They're escalating their tactics." She shakes her head.

The thugs start showing up every day. And not just to shout. Now they pass out leaflets to anyone who'll have them. The handouts say *Stamp Out the Mexican Invasion – Keep America White*. I haven't seen many people take the propaganda — what Daddy calls it — but some do, and a few give a thumbs-up when they read it.

Mom and I are doing some Saturday baking when GramZees roars into the kitchen. She's been in town to see what the troublemakers are up to. She tosses a bunch of handouts on the counter where I am making rolls for Sunday dinner. "They're plastering this trash all over town!" she fumes. "I pulled these off the telephone poles along Norwood." She shakes her head in disgust. "We got the KKK roaming the streets, and the town council won't put a stop to it! Your friend's right, Blue, the Hate Squad has come to Shortstop." Hate Squad is the name Carla has put to the gang of rabble-rousers.

GramZees is right about the town leaders not doin' anything. When Uncle Ray and his gang first started showing up in front of the hardware store, Mr. Miller put up with it. But when they kept coming, he complained to the mayor that it was driving his customers away. Up to then the mayor and town council had stayed quiet. Even when Mr. Johnson, the *Central Ohio Star* reporter, came to do a second story about the Sunday-morning spectacle, the mayor defended the Hate Squad's presence as "free speech in action." In the interview he told the reporter that, "The preacher's got those illegal Mexicans holed up in his church. I guess others got the right to say they don't like it." The mayor has made it clear that he's "not going to interfere with any group exercising their First Amendment rights."

When Daddy read the mayor's comment in the *Star*, he shook his head. "Not sure the writers of the Constitution intended for 'hate speech' to be included in the 'free speech' amendment," he said. Then he added that the mayor probably agrees with the hateful things the white supremacists say, so that makes it "free" by the mayor's accounting.

After Mr. Miller spoke up, other store owners said the protests were costing them money too, so the mayor and the town council finally decided to take action. They had a talk with Uncle Ray, or at least that's what Rev. Adams thinks happened. Clearly some deal was struck, because on Friday afternoon, Uncle Ray unexpectedly repositioned his band of hooligans in front of the church, away from the money-making businesses.

The merchants are happy with the new location, and the mayor has gone back to his defense of the First Amendment. Apparently, "free speech" can go on in Shortstop as long as store owners don't lose money. Anyone on church business has to get past the Hate Squad gauntlet first, and we are not looking forward to church tomorrow. But we are all going, even Mom and Daddy. "We gotta show our solidarity with the Methodists," Daddy says. "They're tryin' to do what they think is right."

CHAPTER 25

"The MYF slumber party is still on!" Connie calls me with the news. The event was in doubt after the uptick of the Hate Squad activity caused some parents to question the wisdom of the church overnighter. In the end, the adults decided they wouldn't "let hate win," as Mr. Taylor put it. Church activities, including the slumber party, would go on as usual. But the MYF parents did think to take the extra precaution to beef up the chaperone list for the party. The MYF kids groaned when we heard that part, but here's the good side of it: Alice and Ted are going to be there as part of the beef-up. Rev. Adams asked them to "babysit" Elenita and César at the church for the night. Now Dolores is free to join in all the fun *and* Alice and Ted will be at the party.

We only have a week to pull everything together, so Connie calls an emergency planning meeting. "I've got a great idea to kick off the slumber party!" Carla whoops. Mom is arranging zinnias in a vase on the coffee table, and the Cs and I are sprawled on the living room floor. Carla's got our attention. "The whole MYF could meet up Friday night at the drug store," she says. "We'll each get one of Mr. Willie's amazing sundaes." Her eyes sparkle at the thought. "Then we walk to the church together and 'let the games begin!'" She rubs her hands in anticipation.

"Might work." Connie is cautious. "Who *doesn't* like Mr. Willie's sundaes?"

"Good idea," I say, "but one big problem."

The Cs turn to look at me. "What?" Carla's a little offended.

"Dolores can't go," I answer.

"Oh, right," the Cs say in unison.

"I completely forgot she can't leave the church." Carla lightly smacks her forehead. "But maybe we could sneak them out." She doesn't want to let go of the plan.

"Not a good idea," I say. "Too risky."

"What a bummer," Carla concedes. "Oh, well." She lets it go.

"It was a great idea," Connie and I say together.

"It still is." Mom surprises us.

And that's how Mom, Daddy, and GramZees get into the ice cream business—at least for one night. They agree to set up a mini ice cream shop in the church basement on Friday night. They promise to bring everything we need to make sundaes, including lots of drippy toppings, chopped nuts, and whipped cream. GramZees suggests taking a few bananas for anyone who wants to go whole hog. Turns out Mr. Willie says he'll donate all the ice cream and loan out his dippers. And he'll throw in a jar of his reddest cherries.

The Friday night ice cream kickoff is a winner! And the rest of the slumber party goes off without a hitch. The Hate Squad stays away—maybe to hate someone else instead. And Jimmy comes, which is a huge surprise. And he beats Gary *and* Rev. Adams at Skittles—an even bigger surprise. Dolores tries to stay up all night, like the rest of us, to eat popcorn and cookies till she's almost sick—also like the rest of us. And Elenita and César fall in love with the Harlans.

After little Edith and baby Teddy go to sleep, Ted carries César around on his shoulders until the boy is too tired to hold on. "He misses Papá," Dolores whispers to me when she sees how happy César is. Elenita hangs on the sidelines looking lost, until Alice pulls balls of bright-colored yarn out of her giant purse along with two large crochet needles. Elenita sparkles when she sees the funny crooked needles, and after a few lessons, she quickly masters the chain stitch.

Alice and Elenita work side by side to create thick multi-colored crochet-ropes. As the slumber party goes on, Elenita's rope-chain grows longer and longer. By the time she puts down her crochet needle, her chain stretches almost from one side of the room to the other. The two sewing buddies decide to twirl the colored chains around their necks like scarves.

"¡Baile mexicano!" Elenita laughs as she and Alice flip their scarves and flare their skirts in a pretend Mexican dance around the room. Elenita takes the lead and shows Alice some basic steps. Several of us, including Dolores, join in.

"I love to dance!" Alice laughs and collapses into a chair when they are done. "An' crochet," she adds. "My granny taught me to make chains when I was just a snip. Elenita picked it up real fast," she brags to Dolores.

"An' now you dance like a mexicana," Dolores compliments her.

"Your sister's a good teacher." Alice throws a thank-you kiss to Elenita.

CHAPTER 26

"The abuela is not Abuela." Rev. Adams gives us the bad news, perched on the edge of the davenport in our front room. The rest of us are gathered around to hear what he's come to tell us. After we sent the package to Dave Sagal, we waited to hear back. Now we know that the grandma we all thought would be Dolores, Elenita, and César's Abuela is not.

"Dave says he'll keep digging," Rev. Adams adds hopefully, "but right now he doesn't have any leads." His shrugs in resignation. We are all mute, afraid to expose the greatest fear that hangs in the air: The real Abuela is gone. Maybe deported.

"How long can the kids stay at the church?" Daddy wants to know. It's a big worry for us all.

"As long as they need to," the preacher replies, "but the more urgent concern is how long we can keep them safe there, or anywhere." We all nod. The constant presence of the Hate Squad is more and more alarming. The mob grows every day. Outsiders stream in from all over to take on the "cause" to rid America of the "criminal wetbacks." At times their venomous chants can be heard all the way across the railroad tracks to the other side of town. The mayor and council continue their zealous protection of the First Amendment, and they stand idle as long as Jimmy's uncle keeps the action centered on the church building and doesn't impede town business.

We talk on for the better part of an hour, but we don't find any workable solutions. In the end, we agree to let it rest for a day or two in hopes that Dave Sagal can work some miracle in Melard. "He's still trying to locate the grandmother," Rev. Adams reminds us when we part.

The miracle comes, but not from Dave Sagal.

"Exciting news!" Rev. Adams comes knocking before nine in the morning. He bursts into the kitchen as soon as Mom opens the door. He can hardly keep still. "Sorry to barge in. I tried to call, but your phone must be off the hook."

"Ahhh! Roscoe again!" Mom shakes her head. "Darn cat knocks the receiver off when he jumps to the window. I think he does it on purpose. Sorry."

"Doesn't matter." Rev. Adams rushes ahead. "I had to come this way anyway to see Mr. Knox. He just got home from the hospital. I wanted to tell you to meet me at ten in my office. That reporter, Johnson, and our lawyer, Ms. Linsky, want to talk with us. They've got a lead on the grandmother's whereabouts." We catch his excitement. "The lawyer called me this morning before breakfast. Whatever it is, she doesn't want to talk about it on the phone. Says she and Mr. Johnson will fill us in when they get here."

"Is it good news?" GramZees wants to know.

"Seems so," Rev. Adams says, "but we'll have to wait and see."

"Have you told Dolores, Elenita, and César yet?" I ask.

"I told them as much as I know, but I didn't want to get their hopes up too high." Rev. Adams nods. "Ms. Linsky said they should definitely be at the meeting to learn the news. They are her clients, after all." Rev. Adams smiles. He's halfway out the door and in a rush. Mr. Knox is a talker, and the preacher has a ten o'clock meeting to make. And so do we.

"The pickles will have to wait," Mom says as soon as the preacher leaves. No one complains about a day off from canning as we scurry around to get to the church on time. Mr. Hill rises from his guard chair and jangles his keys. "Morning, folks, the preacher's inside. He's expecting you." He glances at the thuggish men milling around on the sidewalk. "What a bunch of crazies," he mutters under his breath.

The demonstration is just getting organized for the day. Jimmy's uncle welcomes a couple of newcomers, then turns to hand stacks of leaflets to two of the regulars. "Bubba, you cover Norwood. Bobby Jack, you get Main," he barks out his orders. "Don't miss a house. Talk up the rally. We want us a big crowd Saturday."

We know about the weekend rally because the leaflets are plastered all over town. GramZees says the Hate Squad is turning up the heat. "They got the grand poohbah of white supremacists coming in to get people all whipped up," she told us last night. "Folks could end up getting hurt before it's over. Mayor's inviting trouble if he doesn't put a stop to this."

Mr. Hill opens the door and ushers us in as he grumbles on about the "crazies." We are on time for the meeting, but still the last to arrive. Rev. Adams has arranged chairs in a tight circle so we can all sit in his tiny office. "Everyone's here. Let's get started," Ms. Linsky says. "Yesterday, Mr. Johnson contacted me with important information. I have asked him to share it with you. Mr. Johnson, if you'll go ahead, I'll translate."

"This is a strange position for me," he says. "I am usually the person asking for information, not sharing it." He smiles his discomfort. "But I think I have good news about your grandmother." He talks directly to the kids. When Ms. Linsky translates what he says, the kids react immediately. César flashes his sweet grin, Elenita raises her hand to her heart, and Dolores's eyes glisten with tears.

"It all begins with the story I did about you." He pauses. "A lawyer in Melard saw it and was interested. She does a lot of work with immigrants. Kind of like Ms. Linsky." Ms. Linsky nods, but keeps up her fast Spanish. "Turns out the lawyer from Melard knows your grandmother. And, I gather, knows her pretty well." This last part brings smiles all around, and visible relief.

"Now to the heart of it." The reporter pauses. "Your grandmother is safe, but she is hiding. She is very hesitant to come out of the shadows for reasons the lawyer will not say. She has seen your pictures in the *Star*, and she is one hundred percent certain that you are her grandchildren. She is desperate to see you."

With the last words, Dolores, Elenita, and César break into a tearful conversation among themselves. I hear the word "Abuela" over and over, but they are speaking so rapidly, I cannot begin to understand anything else. Ms. Linsky doesn't translate. It's private. But we can hear relief and joy in their voices.

"¿Cuándo podemos ir con mi Abuela?" Dolores asks in Spanish, then English. "When can we go to Abuela?

"The sooner we can get you out of here, the better," says GramZees.

"I agree," Mom says. "That bunch outside scares me."

"We should make the move before the rally on Saturday," Rev. Adams says. "The supremacists are gearing up for a huge crowd, and the mayor and council have let it escalate. The town leaders are not likely to call in the state police to keep things under control. Anything could happen." He's worried like GramZees. "Yep. We need to get the kids out of here before Saturday," the preacher says with determination, "but it will be tricky. They're watching us day and night." He jerks his thumb in the direction of the Hate Squad outside who are at full volume.

Day *and* night? This is alarming information. "What makes you say that?" Ms. Linsky asks for specifics.

"I was up in the bell tower last night," Rev. Adams says. "Rope had gotten twisted and looped over the bell. Anyway, I was up in the tower around ten. There's a slatted air vent in the tower room. You can see out, but no one can see in. It's about eye level with Miller's second floor. At first, I thought I was seeing things. But nope. Big as life, there were two men up there looking over at the church with binoculars."

We are stunned by the creepy discovery.

"You think Mr. Miller knows they're there?" Mom asks.

"I'm not sure if he's in cahoots with them or not," Rev. Adams answers. "Maybe they just found some way in."

"Or maybe that was part of the mayor's deal." GramZees's voice is hard. "Maybe Miller agreed to let the thugs use his second floor to spy on us if they would move away from his front door."

"Could be they struck a deal," Rev. Adams concedes. "But we'll probably never know. We *do* know that that gang of hoodlums is keeping tabs of every move we make. And if they spot the kids off the church property, they will try to take them."

I am doubly glad we held our ice cream shop in the church basement. Ms. Linsky has stopped translating, which is for the best, I think. Dolores has understood the gist of the threat. Her face is pale. Elenita watches her for clues.

"Está bien. No te preocupes," Dolores reassures Elenita. "It's okay. Don't worry." I hope that's true.

Later in the afternoon, I meet up with the Cs at the R & R for Coca-Cola and pretzels. We want to finalize transportation plans for the Cedar Point trip. We leave Friday morning and come back late Saturday.

"I'm glad we're not going to be here for the Hate Rally," Carla says. Connie and I agree.

"I wish Dolores and the kids could come to Cedar Point with us," Connie laments. We've had this discussion before at the MYF meeting—everyone wants them to come—but they can't leave the church property or they will be "out of sanctuary," Rev. Adams explained.

This morning's revelations underlined how dangerous leaving the church could be. We understand the threat even better, now that we know that spies are watching every move with binoculars. I don't mention any of this to Connie and Carla, because I am sworn to secrecy. "Loose lips sink ships," GramZees, of course, reminded us all. We parted the morning meeting without a plan to safely get our sanctuary family to their grandmother, but we did agree that we'd sleep on it.

And I do. The danger to Dolores, Elenita, and César is the last thing on my mind when I drift off to sleep and first thing that jumps into my head in the morning. And as soon as I open my eyes, I know how we can slip our Mexican family past the Hate Squad spies. I got the idea from *Armchair Theatre*. Last night's movie was a true story about Catholic nuns in WWII. The nuns took a Jewish family into their convent to hide them from the Nazis. That worked fine for a while, but the Nazi soldiers were everywhere spying on everyone, including the nuns. The Jewish family needed to get out of Germany to be really safe. At first, it seemed impossible to sneak the family over the border undetected, but the smart nuns had a plan. They dressed the family up in black, swishy nun outfits and sneaked them past the enemy soldiers in plain sight.

"I know what to do!" I announce as soon as I burst into the kitchen. "I know how to get Dolores and the kids out of the church and off to their abuela!" Everyone is around the table, even Daddy, who hasn't left for work yet.

"We're all ears, Blue." I think Daddy is teasing me a little. "But maybe you should have your coffee first. I don't think you're excited enough." Now I know he's teasing.

"No, really, I have a great idea," I defend myself. But I do pour some coffee before I launch into a description of my plan.

"Could work." GramZees nods when I'm done explaining. "But we don't have any nuns' outfits." Now *she's* teasing me. Mom has a smile and I can see she likes the idea. Daddy too.

"There's a lot of pieces to fit together," Mom says, "and it's already the middle of the week. Everything has to be ready by Friday. We need to talk to the others as soon as possible."

We get to the church even before the Hate Squad begins to assemble. Mr. Hill unlocks the door and lets us in to find Rev. Adams in his office waiting for us. We called ahead. "Blue has a plan that we think might work to sneak all three kids out undetected and get them to their grandmother up in Melard," Mom says.

CHAPTER TWENTY-SIX

Rev. Adams nods. He's eager to hear.

Mom motions for me to begin. I launch into a rundown of the hiding-in-plain-sight idea.

"It'll be tricky to pull this off," Rev. Adams says slowly after I outline the basic plan, "but I think it might work." I hear resolve in his voice. He jumps to details. "We'll need to split the kids into two cars, and mix the vehicles in with all the others headed to Cedar Point." Rev. Adams shakes his head. "And my car can't be one of them. I'm pretty sure the spies are watching me especially close."

"Daddy says to count him in to help," I pass on the message.

"He said he will take off work if he needs to," Mom adds, "and I'm sure he'd volunteer to drive one of the cars."

"I think Ted and Alice will want to help too," Rev. Adams says. "They have taken a real liking to the kids, and they have their own car now that Ted got on out at GM. Also, they have a lot of sympathy for the parents. Ted says the big difference between the Mexican family and his family is that he and Alice didn't have immigration police chasing them when they came north to find work."

"What about two or three MYF kids?" GramZees asks. "We need them to ride in the cars with Dolores and the kids so everything looks normal. Just a bunch of church families headed to Cedar Point." GramZees is warming to the idea. "Who would be best to ask? For sure only kids who can absolutely keep a secret," she adds.

"We know, GramZees," I say. "'Loose lips sink ships.'" We all laugh. GramZees takes it in good humor.

"Well, it's true." She smiles sheepishly. We get back to the question about which MYF kids to bring on to our team. Everyone turns to me.

"Connie and Carla, for sure," I say. There's lots of quick agreement. I pause before I make my final suggestion. "I think the other MYF person should be Jimmy." The others are silent.

"Why Jimmy?" Rev. Adams finally asks.

"Jimmy wants to make things right," I say simply. "This would be his chance."

"But," GramZees interjects, "can we trust him? He's told on us before. It's a big risk." She clearly doesn't like the idea. "Maybe he's being friendly with Dolores and the kids just to throw us off. And maybe he joined the MYF to find out things for his uncle." There, she said it. Maybe Jimmy is a spy. The fear has been knocking around in my head ever since he showed up unexpectedly for the slumber party.

No one speaks as we consider the serious charge GramZees has put on the table.

Mom is the first to break the silence. "I've known Jimmy since he was little, and his family too. Jimmy made a mistake when he told his uncle about us. I think he knows that now. I believe he is truly sorry for what he did."

"We can forgive him for what he did," GramZees pushes back, "but I'm not sure we should risk including him now. It's Dolores, Elenita, and César who would pay the price if we are wrong."

"Then they should decide," I suggest.

"They need to decide about all of this," Rev. Adams says quietly. "Let's go talk to them."

We adjourn our meeting and head upstairs to Dolores, Elenita, and César's "house."

GramZees carefully explains the hiding-in-plain-sight getaway plan in Spanish. Elenita and César like the idea that they will be with their new friends, Ted and Alice. César is especially excited that he might get to ride in Ted's big red car. "Gran carro rojo!" He beams. Up to now, he has been able to admire the long, shiny Chevy Bel Air only through the church window. It is a snazzy looking car, and Ted says he got a really good deal because he works at GM.

Dolores has more serious concerns. She likes the idea of asking Connie and Carla, but she hesitates on Jimmy. She has gotten to know him pretty well through the slumber party and the other times he has come with me to hang out, but she also knows the rest of his story that makes him a risk. We turn over the pros and cons. Finally, she decides. "Todos merecen una segunda oportunidad."

"Everyone deserves a second chance," GramZees translates. It's settled. Jimmy will be a part of the travel team.

That decided, Dolores wants to know how we will actually make contact with their abuela when we get to Melard. It's a good question. "Right now, I am not sure," Rev. Adams answers. "I will ask Ms. Linsky to make the arrangements through your grandmother's lawyer friend — the one who contacted Mr. Johnson after she saw his article. She definitely knows where your grandmother is."

Dolores nods her agreement. She sits quietly for a moment, then she turns toward us and in perfect English she says, "Okay, gang! Let's roll!" She grins mischievously as she delivers the line. She learned it at the slumber party.

"Okay, gang," Rev. Adams picks it up with a smile. "Let's make plans. I think Melard and Cedar Point are not too far apart." Rev. Adams spreads an Ohio map across the tabletop. We all circle around.

"Look at this," he says as he traces his finger over the maze of lines, "it's even better than I thought. We'll pass right through Melard on the way to Cedar Point. The MYF trip is the perfect cover!" He smacks his hand down on top of the map and looks up at us.

Mom reminds us that we have to move fast to get everything into place by Friday morning when the MYF leaves for Cedar Point. Our strategy is to hide Dolores, Elenita, and César in with the MYF kids loading for departure. The risky part is getting them from the building into the waiting cars without being noticed by the "watchers." We hope a bunch of excited kids milling around will create enough diversion to throw off any spies. But just in case, I have a secret backup idea.

According to our plan, Dolores, the Cs, and I will be in Daddy's car. Elenita and César will ride with Ted and Alice, their "parents" for the day. GramZees and Jimmy will also ride in the big red Chevy. Six is a lot, but the Bel Air can easily handle it, Rev. Adams assures us. The preacher will drive his car with Ms. Linsky and Mr. Johnson inside. The reporter has made a strong argument to be included. He wants to do a follow-up story on the family's reunion if the grandmother agrees to be interviewed.

Rev. Adams says he will call Ms. Linsky and ask her to contact the lawyer in Melard to set up a safe rendezvous time and location on Friday. Then he'll drive to Mudsock to talk with Ted and Alice.

My job is to get Connie, Carla, and Jimmy on board. I start with the easier task, and as soon as the meeting is over, I call the Cs to meet me at the R & R. We find a back corner where no one will bother us or hear us. I lay out the basic hide-in-plain-sight-get-out-of-town idea. They think it's wicked-smart, and I take a millisecond to bask in the glow of my brilliance. But then we are back to business.

"Count me in," Carla says.

"Me too," Connie echoes. "We can ride with Dolores, but if we are going to fool the Hate Squad, she's got to look just like the rest of us." Connie looks serious.

"You're right," I agree. I'm not sure what Connie's got in mind, but she's running with an idea.

"I've only seen her wear skirts and blouses," Connie says. "Does Dolores have any pedal pushers or Keds?" I shake my head no. Dolores doesn't wear short pants like the rest of us girls. And she doesn't have any laced canvas shoes either. I look down at the red Keds I'm wearing. Dolores always wears flats.

"So, no pedal pushers or Keds," Connie summarizes, "that's what I figured, but we can fix that." The clothes for the disguise are settled, at least in Connie's mind. She moves to the next topic. "Dolores has great hair—it's so black and silky." I can tell Connie's doing the make-over in her head. "I bet she'd look super with her hair up in a ponytail like all the girls are wearing now." Connie's turned fashion consultant *and* hairdresser. Carla and I just laugh, but Connie's right about giving Dolores a new look to fool the Hate Squad spies. We've got to consider a new look for Elenita too. And probably César. He can get by with a baseball cap and a Cincinnati Reds T-shirt. All the boys are wearing them around town.

The Cs and I part after an hour and two Cokes with pretzels. We each have our "marching orders," as Connie calls them. Her uncle was in the military. Connie's in charge of consulting with Dolores and Elenita about the disguises and then assembling everything that's needed. She'll also offer to do the ponytails. Carla has a cousin about César's size, so she will borrow clothes from him. She thinks her cousin is a Cincinnati Reds fan. All the better.

I have the hardest marching order: talk with Jimmy. I so hope I have not made a mistake by suggesting him. I split off from my friends outside the R & R and start down Norwood Street toward home. Halfway there, I spot Jimmy. He's on the other side of the street coming toward me heading into town. Great luck! "Hey, Jimmy," I yell and wave. "Got a minute?"

"Sure, Blue, whad'ya want?" He crosses over and comes up beside me. He's all smiles, so that's good.

"Let's go to our hideout." I just blurt it out. He starts to object but stops.

"Okay," he agrees without another word, and we cut over on a side street to the railroad tracks. We walk in silence atop the gravel railroad bed past the apple orchard to our secret place in the scrubby trees. We both know that today is not about apples or smoking cigarettes. It's about talking in private, away from prying ears and spying eyes.

"So, what's up, Blue?" he asks when we are settled with our backs against the biggest of the struggling saplings in our hideout. I take a deep breath and launch right into it.

"I'm going to tell you a huge secret, Jimmy, but first you gotta promise that you will not repeat it. Not to anyone. If you do, a lot of people could get hurt. Do you understand?" I want him to know from the beginning that the stakes are high.

"I won't tell, Blue," he says, all solemn. "If it's about Dolores, Elenita, and César—and I think it is—I promise that I will protect them, and I will never do anything that will put them in danger again."

"Okay," I say slowly. He's said what I need to hear. I just hope he's not lying.

I begin with the *Armchair Theater* movie about the nuns and the Jewish family's escape. Jimmy looks a little bewildered in the beginning, but then he starts to get it. I lay out the general hide-in-plain-sight ruse and he immediately knows I'm talking about getting Dolores, Elenita, and César past the "enemy lines" of his uncle's Hate Squad. I didn't set out to do it, but I end up telling Jimmy the long story about the family's run from la Migra raids in Texas, the harrowing train trip in the boxcar, their parents getting "disappeared" in Chicago, the "bad man" who caused them to hide in the garden shed, the days eating raw corn scavenged from our garden, and finally the grandmother in Melard who Dolores, Elenita, and César so desperately want to find. I go over how we will use the MYF Cedar Point trip as the cover to get them safely out of town.

And finally, I get to his part. "We want you to ride with César and Elenita in Ted and Alice's car — sort of like you're an older brother," I say.

"That's easy." Jimmy smiles. "They're great kids. And I've kinda turned into their older brother." He grins proudly.

"That's all true," I say, "but there's more. A lot more that I want you to do." I pause.

Jimmy turns serious. "Ooooh Kaaaaay. What is it?"

"I want you to distract your Uncle Ray, keep him busy, while we make the switch from the church to the cars. The kids will dress to blend in, but we don't want to take any chances. Once they're off the church property, anyone who wants to can hurt them." I stop.

Jimmy is quiet. He knows I mean his uncle.

"And we're sure we're being spied on," I say deliberately. If Jimmy knows about the upstairs window and the binoculars, he doesn't show it.

"We won't let Uncle Ray find out," Jimmy says softly. "Leave it to me, Blue, I know how to get Uncle Ray's attention. By the time he figures out what's happened, Dolores, Elenita, and César will be out of his reach."

CHAPTER 27

"¡Veremos a nuestra abuela el viernes! We will see our grandmother on Friday!" Dolores hugs Elenita and César. Their eyes dance with the thought of it. It's Thursday afternoon, and Rev. Adams, GramZees, and I have come to deliver good news to Dolores and her siblings.

The lawyer in Melard got back within a day, and Ms. Linsky called Rev. Adams straightaway with the instructions. When we arrive in Melard on Friday, we are to go to the church where Dave Sagal is pastor. Abuela's immigration lawyer will meet us there around noon. If everything checks out, she will take us to the grandmother, who is waiting anxiously to hug her lost grandchildren.

It will take about two hours to get to Melard, and the timing works perfectly with the MYF Cedar Point departure. Parent drivers, chaperones, and MYF kids will converge on the church at nine-thirty to load up for a ten o'clock blast-off.

We all chat a bit more, then Rev. Adams and GramZees leave. I hang around because Dolores wants to show me their disguises. The Cs worked fast to gather two pairs of pedal pushers, one for Dolores and one for Elenita; three pairs of Keds in appropriate sizes, and a Cincinnati Reds baseball cap and T-shirt which César wants to keep because red is his favorite color. Carla assures him she can "make it happen." Everyone is nervous about tomorrow, but I think we are ready.

We have a mostly sleepless night at our house but get up on Friday alert from adrenaline. Mom has a good breakfast ready, but we don't do it justice. We eat hurriedly, then bolt out the door. Daddy parks our black Chevy at the curb directly across from the side church door. We have come a little early to get the curb spaces closest to the building. Ted's Bel Air glides in behind us. He and Alice came to our house around eight-thirty to get Edith and Little Teddy settled in with Mom for the day, then followed us to the church.

Mr. Hill hails us when we get out of the car, and steps over to speak briefly with Daddy to let him know he's keeping a watch on things. Rev. Adams brought him in on the plan. Mr. Hill has seen the Hate Squad crowd close up day after day, and he will be good at spotting any suspicious changes in their morning routine.

The Hate Squad is beginning to assemble, and Uncle Ray scurries around handing out the posters and leaflets about tomorrow's rally. He's pushing hard to get a big crowd. I take a quick glance up at Miller's second floor. I don't see any binoculars aimed our way, but who knows? The spies could be anywhere.

Ted gets out of the Bel Air to unlock his trunk and throw up the lid like the other parents. Then he stands beside his car to wait. Alice gets out too, and GramZees walks over to chat. As per our plan, Alice announces to anyone who might be listening that she has to pee before they start the trip. She walks to the church building, and Mr. Hill opens the door to let her pass.

Jimmy has assured me that he will show up in time to distract his uncle while we make our move. We plan to hustle Dolores and the kids into the cars at the last minute, because the less exposure to prying eyes, the less chance of detection.

More cars arrive, and MYF kids pile out to join the excited group already gathered on the sidewalk. Parents mill together making small talk while they wait. Trunk lids stand open and kids throw in lunch sacks, thermos bottles and extra bags of potato chips for the trip. Hate Squad thugs roll into town too and compete with parents and MYF kids for the sidewalk space. The groups don't interact, but they keep a wary eye on each other. At one point, Uncle Ray tries to get some MFY kids to take his leaflets, but Mr. Jackson, Gary's dad, moves quickly between them and waves him away.

Frustrated, Uncle Ray walks down the line of cars parked at the curb. He tries to talk up the rally with the waiting adults who either ignore him or politely shake their heads no to send him on his way. When he gets to our car, he stops and takes a hard look. His cold stare sends shivers over my whole body. "You live a couple houses from my brother-in-law, doncha?" he asks Daddy. It's an accusation. Not friendly. "Baxter, right?" Despite his demeanor, he shoves his hand out for Daddy to shake.

"Yep." Daddy just nods and keeps his arms folded across his chest as he leans against the Chevy.

"And you're good friends with my nephew, Jimmy," he says deliberately as he turns his attention to me. It has dawned on him that we are the ones who hid the "dirty Mexican kids."

"Yep," I reply, "I know Jimmy." I keep my answer short. I want Uncle Ray to leave. It's almost time to get our special passengers loaded up, and I don't want him to focus attention on us. Suspicion squirts from his squinty eyes.

"Hey, Uncle Ray." Jimmy appears unexpectedly from behind. His uncle spins around to face him. "Ya got a minute? I got some important stuff I need to talk to you about."

"Now?" Uncle Ray barks.

"Yeah," Jimmy says. "It can't wait." Jimmy jerks his head to the side. He wants his uncle to follow him. "We need to talk in private." He lowers his voice.

But Uncle Ray's not buying it. "Not now, Jimmy, I'm in the middle of something here." He glances back at us.

"Remember what we talked about the other day?" Jimmy tries to lure him. "Well, I got stuff to tell ya. And it can't wait, okay?" Jimmy holds his uncle's gaze, trying to communicate the urgency.

Uncle Ray's lips slowly slip into a grim-line smile. "Okay, let's walk down a couple of blocks." Suddenly he's all interested. Seems Jimmy has information to share. Daddy, GramZees, and I exchange a fearful glance.

"I hope we didn't make a mistake in trusting him," GramZees mutters under her breath.

"Me too," I whisper grimly. But there's no time to second guess. Rev. Adams appears from the front of the church and makes his way down the sidewalk toward his car. He stops to chat several times along the way. We know he's checking the crowd for unfamiliar faces to spot possible spies. When he reaches his car, he takes one last long look around, then nods his head slightly before he gets in the driver's seat. His nod is the go signal.

Alice and the Cs have been watching the preacher through the window from inside the church building. Now they have the all-clear, so they know it's time. Alice emerges from the side door with Dolores right behind her. Her disguise is so good, it's hard to believe she's not just one of the Shortstop MYF crowd. Elenita and César follow close behind with Connie on one side and Carla on the other to partially shield them from view. Again, the transformation is remarkable. Elenita could be any eight-year-old in town, and César looks like he just got home from a Reds game. Ms. Linsky and Mr. Johnson quickly move into place beside them to add extra cover.

The trip to the cars goes smoothly and quickly according to plan. Connie and Carla fall into place as soon as Dolores is in the back seat of Daddy's Chevy. Ted has the doors open on the Bel Air, and GramZees and Alice hurriedly shuffle César and Elenita into the car. Ms. Linsky and Mr. Johnson peel away and make their way to Rev. Adams's sedan parked at the curb several cars ahead of us. The preacher's car will take the lead out of town. It's ten o'clock and we need to go.

"Where's Jimmy?" Ted asks as he looks around. Jimmy's not in the Bel Air, and there's no sight of him on the sidewalk. We haven't seen him since he scurried away with Uncle Ray. "Should we leave 'im?" Ted poses the question. "The longer the wait, the more we risk," he adds.

"One more minute," Daddy allows. Rev. Adams has opened his door and stepped out to glance back at us. He is wondering what the delay is. He and the others in his car don't know about the conversation on the sidewalk between Jimmy and Uncle Ray. Traitor Jimmy could be spilling his guts right now.

"Here he comes," Ted says. He throws up a hand to the preacher to give the okay, and heads for the driver's seat as Jimmy jumps into the fancy red car beside César. Rev. Adams immediately eases his car away from the curb, and Daddy and Ted fall in behind him. The other MYF drivers streamed out a few minutes ahead of us with Mr. Taylor in the lead. He knows to go on to Cedar Point without us.

We hardly breathe until we are well out of town and in route to Melard. Daddy and I keep checking to make sure no strange cars are following us. Rev. Adams has dropped back, and Daddy says he can't see him in the rearview mirror any longer. It's a little worrisome. "Hope the preacher's not having car trouble," Daddy wonders. But there's nothing to do but keep going and meet up again in Melard. Daddy and Ted both have the church address and our cars are sticking pretty close together for the moment. We have the "precious cargo," as GramZees calls it.

As the miles go on without incident, we relax a bit. It's a beautiful day with just a hint of fall color in the trees. It seems early in the season for the leaves to turn, but it is almost Labor Day, so not totally unexpected. I ohh and ahh at the colors and chat intermittently with the Cs and Dolores, but my mind is on Jimmy. Did he tell his uncle our plan? The farther we get from Shortstop without trouble, the more convinced I am that he did not. But it sure sounded like he was going to, so maybe. I vacillate. I believe in my friend, and then I don't.

"We're about halfway," Daddy breaks into my thoughts. "Keep your eyes open for a filling station, Blue. We're gonna need gas pretty soon. And a stop will give Ted and the preacher time to catch up to us." We lost sight of Ted's Bel Air not too far out of Shortstop. Maybe he slowed up to check on Rev. Adams.

"Sure," I say, "but it might be awhile before we find a station. Not much around here but fields."

"Maybe in Bucyrus," Daddy says. "It's a fair-sized town. We'll try to make it there if we have to. I sure don't want to run out of gas."

Luckily, I spot a Sinclair station before it comes to that. "There's a green Dino comin' up," I call out to Daddy.

Dino the Dinosaur is the Sinclair Gas logo, and I can see one ahead stuck up in the middle of a soybean field.

"Glad to find a filling station so far out," Daddy says as he slows down to pull in. "Kinda strange, though. Maybe the farmers need it so they don't have to go into town." He thinks it through. "But no farmers now." He glances around. "Or anyone else either." Daddy's a little uneasy. Ten, maybe fifteen miles back, we thought we spotted someone on our tail. The car finally dropped out of sight, so we figured it turned off, but we kept our eyes on the mirrors for a while after.

The station looks deserted, but when our car rolls over the bell hose, a skinny teenager with bad skin wanders out. "Fill 'er up," Daddy says through the window. The pimply-faced kid nods without a word, unscrews the gas cap and starts the pump. Daddy opens his door and eases out of the driver's seat to stretch. He unfolds the Ohio map across the front hood while the kid slow-washes the back window glass. The teenager glances down the empty highway like he's expecting someone.

As soon as Daddy gets out, Carla swings open the back door in a rush. "I'm sooo glad we stopped. I'm about to burst!" She bolts from the car and heads straight for the "Ladies" sign hanging on the far side of the concrete station office. Connie, Dolores, and I fall into step and follow her around the corner.

The ladies room is so small it can accommodate only one person, so we have to take our time. We let Carla go first and the rest of us stretch and chatter while we wait. It feels good to be out of the cramped car, and we relax a bit. The cold anxiety from the morning has begun to melt. When we've each had our turn, we start slowly back toward the car. Our mood is lighter the farther from Shortstop we go and the closer we get to Melard. I walk up beside Dolores. "Almost there," I tell her. She smiles a beautiful smile. I reach for her hand. We round the corner of the building together...

Uncle Ray is waiting for us!

Daddy is nowhere in sight, but I can hear him yelling and kicking from the trunk. Uncle Ray leans against the side of our Chevy, and two scruffy men stand on either side of him. One is huge and hairy like a gorilla, and I've seen him at the Hate rallies. The other is Bobby Jack, the man who threatened Rev. Adams on TV.

"Ahh, there you are." Uncle Ray stares through us. His face is locked and hard. "Guess that little Mexican brat isn't in 'sanctuary' no more." He spits out "sanctuary" like it's a piece of rotten meat.

Jimmy's uncle straightens and takes a step in our direction. "Now, you can come with us peaceable," he points toward Dolores, "or we can rough you up some. Either way we're takin' ya." He raises his eyebrows and lowers his chin to let us know he means it.

"We've been tellin' ya," he says in a mocking voice, "we don't want ya here." He moves closer. "We warned ya." Another step toward us. "This country's got no place for dirty Mexicans." He jabs his finger at us. "We've come ta clean up the trash." Uncle Ray directs his hateful words at Dolores. She doesn't understand it all, but she knows the intent: Another bad man wants to hurt her.

When Uncle Ray steps away from the car, Gorilla Man and Bobby Jack follow his lead and fan out to the sides. I look around, frantically searching for help or a place for us to hide. The pimple-faced kid is nowhere in sight, and the station's front door is shut and the pulled-down shade says "CLOSED." Maybe the skinny kid's inside. Maybe he'll call the sheriff. Maybe he's part of the ambush. Maybe... maybe...

We could make for the soybean fields around us, but there's no cover there. We'd get separated, and Dolores would be totally unprotected while the thugs pick us off one by one. We have to make our stand together. It's our best hope. Our only hope. Without saying a word, the Cs and I grab hands to make a tight circle around Dolores. We face out to defend ourselves as best we can from the attack we know is coming.

The three men descend on us. "I see you girls are gonna make things hard." Uncle Ray rubs his hands together. "Okie dokie, if that's the way you want it." He flashes a satisfied smirk and takes a menacing step closer. He's wanted this for weeks.

"Go away! Leave us alone!" I say low, like a cat's growl warning a predator.

"Ain't you feisty? I like that." Bobby Jack grabs my arm. Like a flash, Carla's left foot smashes his shin dead-on. The blow catches him off guard, and he jumps sideways within Connie's reach. She lands a targeted kick high between his legs. He grabs himself and doubles over, temporarily out of commission.

"Little girls beatin' up on you, Bobby Jack?" Uncle Ray taunts.

"We oughta' lynch the whole lot of 'em," Bobby Jack lashes back weakly. He's still doubled in pain. We've made a fool of him. "The white ones too," he snarls. "They ain't no better than the dirty Mexican they're protectin'."

"They ain't no real Americans, that's for damn sure," Gorilla Man joins in. The guy's huge — a good three inches taller and a hundred pounds heavier than either of the other two.

"You got that right, Bubba!" Bobby Jack nods to the hairy gorilla. He's getting back his swagger. "C'mon, let's get this done." He stands up straight. "We know what we're here to do. Let's stop pussy-footin' around." Bobby Jack and Bubba look to Uncle Ray.

Their leader nods slightly to give the go-ahead. "Let's get to it," he says calmly.

"That's what I been waitin' ta hear!" Bubba grabs me and yanks sideways. Like a snake strike, I sink my teeth into his hairy arm, and I don't let go until I taste blood.

"You little witch!" he screams and draws his fist back to hit me.

"STOP IT! STOP IT RIGHT NOW!" A frantic shout comes from nowhere, but I know the voice. It's Jimmy and he's racing toward us, yelling all the way. Ted is right behind him and GramZees a close third. I never knew she could move so fast.

CHAPTER 28

---

immy's shouts stop Bubba's fist in mid-air. The thug trio spins around to face the new challengers. "Well, well. It's Jimmy and all his new friends," Uncle Ray sneers at his nephew. "Thought ya had me fooled, didn't ya? You little lying piece of sh—"

"What's going on here?" GramZees interrupts with force. Her hands splay on her hips in a don't-mess-with-me stance. Uncle Ray redirects his attention to my grandmother. Her eyes blaze at him.

"We're just having us a friendly discussion with these young ladies," he says sarcastically. "They're interferin' with a citizen's arrest. We're takin' custody of that wetback kid." He points his head toward Dolores. "We'll just get that dirty little Mexican in our car, and we'll be on our way." He moves to take hold of Dolores. "And while we're at it, we'll take those other two wetbacks." He points toward Elenita and César who are standing by the side of the Bel Air. Alice has hold of their hands, not sure what to do. "Nice that you brought 'em along," he sneers.

"No!" Jimmy steps in front of his uncle. "No! You can't take any of them!" Jimmy's in his uncle's face.

"And who's gonna stop me?" Uncle Ray looks around with a smirk on his face. "A wobbly old woman and a bunch of kids?" He figures Bobby Jack and the gorilla can make quick work of Ted. He might be right. "This is a bona fide citizen's arrest, so get out of the way." Uncle Ray shoves Jimmy aside. "Bubba," take care of that 'un." He nods toward Ted. "Bobby Jack. Go get the other two Mexicans," Uncle Ray barks and jerks his head in the direction of the red Bel Air. It's parked next to Daddy's car.

Our old Chevy sits where Daddy parked it. It's dark and eerily silent. The sounds from the trunk have stopped. "DADDY!" I scream and take off in a run. "Daddy's in the trunk! He can't breathe!" I am desperate.

Ted sidesteps Bubba and shoots ahead of me like a rocket. "I got it!" he yells over his shoulder in a sprint. All attention is on the Chevy...and on another car that squeals to a stop beside it. Three occupants jump out: Rev. Adams, Ms. Linsky, and reporter Johnson. Our odds just got better. Uncle Ray has lost control of the situation.

Ted gets the Chevy trunk open, but for a scary moment nothing changes. Then Ted reaches in, and another hand lifts from the trunk to grasp it. Daddy's head appears, and the rest of him follows as he unfolds himself from the cramped space. Dried blood crusts a big gash on his forehead and his left eye's headed toward black, but mostly Daddy's okay. I know, because his hug is the same as always. "Daddy! Daddy! Daddy!" It's all I can get out. I am so relieved.

"You all okay, Blue?" Daddy whispers in my ear. "I was so worried." He turns and pins Uncle Ray in his gaze. "I won't let this go," he snarls. I have never seen Daddy so angry. His warning hits its mark. But we've got more immediate worries. A police siren is wailing in the distance, and it's headed our direction.

I glance at Dolores, Elenita, and César. They are rigid and wild-eyed with fear. They have been running from the law for weeks, and now the law is upon them.

A sheriff's car screeches into the Sinclair station, and a lone deputy gets out. His hand rests lightly on a holstered gun, and he takes in every detail as he walks slowly toward us.

"Hey, man, you finally got here!" The deputy whirls around with his gun drawn. The skinny, pimple-faced kid has jogged up behind him. "Whoa! Hold on, man." The kid throws up his hands. "I'm the one who called."

"Wait inside, son. I'll get to you." The deputy holsters his revolver. "Next time don't come up without announcing yourself. You could get yourself shot." The filling station kid retreats as instructed and the deputy returns his attention to us.

"Somebody want to tell me what's going on here?" the officer asks as he looks around the group. His name is Ken Larson, according to the badge pinned on his shirt.

"Deputy Larson, my name is Meredith Linsky." Our lawyer steps forward to take the lead. "I am an attorney, and I represent some of the folks here." She waves a hand in our direction. "What happened is pretty simple. Mr. Baxter," she indicates Daddy, "and these four girls riding in his vehicle stopped for gas and were accosted by these men." She points to Uncle Ray, Bobby Jack, and gorilla man, Bubba.

"Now hold on a minute, Deputy." Uncle Ray lifts up his hand to intervene. "Don't let this fast-talking woman lawyer feed you a bunch of crap. What she's sayin' ain't the story here."

Deputy Larson stops him. "You'll get your turn, Mr... What's your name?"

"Hanes. My name is Hanes," Uncle Ray responds.

"You'll get your turn, Mr. Hanes," the deputy repeats.

"Okay, Deputy, you're in charge." Uncle Ray retreats, still grousing under his breath. "I'm just sayin' it ain't right to let this woman run things." Deputy Larson ignores the intrusion, turns his attention to Ms. Linsky, and nods for her to continue.

"These men overpowered Mr. Baxter, beat him up, and locked him inside the trunk of his car. Then they went after the four girls, one of whom is Mr. Baxter's daughter." She motions me to come forward. "This young lady witnessed it all and can fill in the details you need." She puts me forward as spokesperson to take the spotlight off Dolores. It's a smart move, but a risky one. She's taking a chance that I know not to say too much.

I start the tale with our MYF group and our trip to Cedar Point. I repeat the part about the stop at the Sinclair station for gas, and I end with gorilla Bubba trying to yank me loose from the circle. "That's when I bit him," I say.

The deputy nods. Maybe he thinks it was a good move. I add that Bubba was about to hit me, but Jimmy and the others arrived just in time to stop him. "That's pretty much it," I finish. Ms. Linsky smiles slightly. I told the truth and nothing but the truth, but not all the truth I know.

"So, what's your story, Mr. Hanes?" Deputy Larson nods toward Uncle Ray.

"Well, Deputy, we're just law-abidin' men," he says, and swings his arm to include Bobby Jack and Bubba. "We was tryin to make a citizen's arrest here." Uncle Ray is all chummy. He hopes the deputy is an ally with a badge. "But we'll just go on our way," he moves back a step as he talks, "now that the real law is on the scene to finish the job." Uncle Ray finishes with a smirky-smile and turns to leave. He wants to make a quick getaway.

"What law has been broken, Mr. Hanes?" Deputy Larson halts the departure with a question. "And who do you think broke it?"

Uncle Ray stops in his tracks. He points to Dolores, then sweeps his hand to include Elenita and César. "Dirty Mexican wetbacks don't belong here," he accuses. "Even Ike says that. White people like us are getting pushed out of our own country. Ain't that right?" He looks directly at the deputy. He expects support. Deputy Larson does not respond.

Uncle Ray goes on: "These...these...people here," he waves his hand toward us, "are hidin' wetbacks—invitin' 'em to supper, lettin' 'em sleep in their beds." Uncle Ray shows his disgust. He pauses. "Look here, Deputy, we was just tryin' to help fine lawmen like you do your job."

"I see," says Deputy Larson. "So, let me get this straight. You and your two friends were trying to arrest these three kids because you believe they are in our country illegally?" He looks intently at Uncle Ray. "And in the process of the attempted arrest, you assaulted this father and locked him in the trunk of his car?" He indicates Daddy. "And then you and your buddies threatened to physically harm the three girls who were protecting the kids you were after? Is that about right, Mr. Hanes?"

"Well, I wouldn't put it exactly like that, Deputy," Uncle Ray counters. "We was jus' helpin' get rid of the illegal scum takin' over our country. Like the president says," he adds weakly. "But, like I say, we'll be on our way. You got the situation handled."

"How about you boys come with me?" Deputy Larson abruptly changes tactics. "I need to get your full statements, but first I want to speak with the young man who reported this situation. You can wait in my cruiser until I'm done." Then he turns to us. "The rest of you stay put. We need to talk some more."

"So, are we going to be okay?" Rev. Adams asks Ms. Linsky as we watch Deputy Larson put Uncle Ray and the other two in his car. He stuffs them into the back seat. The windows are rolled tight. I hope it's blazing hot in there.

"Not sure," the lawyer answers the preacher thoughtfully. "Could go a lot of different ways." Her response is less than reassuring.

With the thugs stashed in the sheriff's cruiser, the Cs and I relax some. We are shaken but tell the others we are okay. Dolores goes to Elenita and César who are still holding tight to Alice's hand. She puts her arms around them and in rapid-fire Spanish tries to explain what's happening.

When Ms. Linsky walks over, Dolores asks if the deputy will take them to jail. "Not if I can help it!" Our lawyer is adamant. "But if he does, I will go with you. I promise," she answers in Spanish. She lays a gentle hand on Dolores's arm.

Daddy, Ted, and the preacher go off to the side to talk, but Jimmy is not with them. He is standing by himself. I break from our group and walk over to him. "Thanks for calling off the gorilla," I say, trying to keep it light. "I think he could've done some damage."

"I expect he would have," Jimmy says, then he blurts, "I didn't tell my uncle, Blue. He just figured it out on his own. I didn't have anything to do with it."

I shrug, not sure what to say.

"My uncle's been trying to get me to spy on you," Jimmy spills it out, "but I kept saying no way. That's how I knew I could keep him off you this morning at the church. I pretended to join up with him. I lied and told him the plan was to make the move on Saturday during the big rally. I figured by the time he found out the truth, everybody would be long gone and safe." Jimmy pauses and looks down. "Guess I figured wrong."

"Maybe one of your uncle's buddies spotted us this morning," I say and shrug again.

"I don't know. Maybe Uncle Ray's just smarter than I thought." He glances up. "Or maybe I'm not as smart as I think." He grins a little at the last part. "Whatever went wrong, I'm sorry it turned out like this, Blue."

Deputy Larson takes a while to interview the kid who pumps gas at the station. The two stay in the filling station office to talk, and when they come out, the deputy goes straight for the radio in his car. I can hear it squawking, but I can't understand what anyone is saying. Deputy Larson relocks the cruiser when he's done and walks in our direction.

"All right, folks, your story checks out with the attendant." The deputy jerks his head toward the skinny teen standing outside by the gas pumps. "He ran inside as soon as the trouble started, but he saw the whole thing through the window and called it in. You're lucky he was here." I feel a twinge of guilt. I haven't given the kid the respect he deserves.

"Now here's the deal," Deputy Larson continues. "I work for the county sheriff's department, not the U.S. Border Patrol. So, you got lucky again because I'm not going dig any deeper here. I got enough to keep me busy without doing the Border Patrol's job too. I may have to call you back to testify on the assault charges," he points toward Daddy, "so I need your phone number, but for now you folks can be on your way." Relief settles over us.

"But," the deputy goes on, "my advice is to load up and hightail it right now. Based on what the witness told me, I'm arresting those fellas," he points toward his locked car, "and I've called for backup to haul them off to the county jail. Probably best if you're not here when the other deputies arrive. They could be nosier than I am."

That's all we need to know. We are back in our cars and on the road to Melard before any more sirens come our way.

CHAPTER 29

I t takes less than an hour to get to Melard, but the delay at the Sinclair station has made us late. We hope that Ms. Dean, the lawyer, is still waiting for us at Rev. Sagal's church as planned. When we arrive, Rev. Adams and Ms. Linsky go inside to check, and Dave Sagal is with them when they return. He's all business. "Pull around to the back, and we'll go in through my office entrance," he tells Daddy through the car window.

Rev. Sagal meets us at the outside office entrance and quickly shepherds Dolores, Elenita, and César inside. The rest of us file in behind. Rev. Sagal's office is bigger than Rev. Adams's, but still won't hold us all. We quickly learn that that's not the plan anyway. Everyone but Ms. Linsky and the three undocumented kids she represents are ushered into another room to wait. After a few minutes, Dave Sagal comes in. "Ms. Dean and Ms. Linsky need time to speak alone with their clients. It's going to take a while," he pauses. "But," he gives us his first smile, "I happen to know where we can find the best fried chicken in Melard. Maybe the best in Ohio. Maybe the best fried chicken in the whole US of A," he brags. "Let's go get some. I'm buying." He grins, clearly more relaxed now that the kids are safely inside.

All ten of us order the fried chicken, and it is as good as promised. Maybe not the best fried chicken in the whole US of A — that's Mom's — but really tasty. After the harrowing day we've had, we are ravenous. Mr. Johnson sits beside Dave Sagal, and they hit it off right away. The reporter pulls his notebook and pen from his shirt pocket and starts writing stuff down. "Background for the story," he explains. He's still angling to do a follow-up piece on the family's reunion with their grandmother.

After an hour-long lunch, we return to the church to say a final good-bye to Dolores, Elenita, and César. We assume the lawyers will take them to their grandmother now, which is, of course, a happy ending to their journey. The great sadness is that they lost their mom and dad in the process — perhaps forever. Dolores fears that they are dead.

"You look like you have a bunch of bees buzzing around in your head." My thoughts must be showing. Jimmy sits down beside me.

"More like hornets," I say and shake my head to get rid of the sound. He nods soberly.

"Me too," he acknowledges, but doesn't say more.

Ms. Linsky appears at the door and walks to the front of the room to get our attention. "Thank you for waiting," she begins. "Everyone's had a long, hard day, but before you go, there is someone who wants to meet you. Dolores will do the introductions." She motions Dolores into the room. Elenita and César follow behind her.

Dolores begins in Spanish, then she stops while Ms. Linsky translates. "This a very sad day and a very happy one. It's is sad because we have to leave all of our new friends behind. You have helped us so much in this hard time. We will never forget your kindnesses." Dolores's voice cracks. My eyes start to drip, and I'm not the only one who needs a Kleenex.

"But as I said, this is a happy day too," Dolores goes on. "Today, after long searching and many difficult problems, we..." But César doesn't wait for his sister to finish. He breaks for the door. A woman stands in the shadows just outside the room talking to Ms. Dean, the other lawyer. He grabs the woman's hand and leads her into the room. I have never seen his biggest smile until now. He beams. And his grandmother beams back.

"May I present to you, la Señora María González Morales, our abuela." Dolores makes the formal introduction. We start clapping...and crying...and clapping some more until Ms. Linsky raises her hand for quiet.

"Señora González Morales has a few words," Ms. Linsky says quietly, then repeats what she said in Spanish. Dolores's grandmother steps closer to us. She is a small woman with glistening black hair parted in the middle and pulled into a back knot. She has a calm gentleness about her that shows even before she speaks.

"Thank you for keeping my grandchildren safe, and thank you for bringing them to me. I was so afraid they were lost forever." Señora González tears up at the thought. She stops talking and holds her hand over her heart. "I have much inside, but no more words to tell you. I just have tears of happiness. Perhaps others can say more." With that, Abuela steps back and looks expectantly toward the door. A man and a woman are standing in the opening beside Ms. Dean.

César cries out, "¡Mamá! ¡Papi!" He bolts for the door. The five-year-old throws his little arms wide open. Papi sweeps his son up onto his shoulders, then throws out his arms to his daughters. Elenita collapses into her dad's embrace. Dolores weeps openly on her mother's shoulder. The rest of us watch in amazement. It is a moment of pure joy. The kids are as surprised as we are by their parents' appearance.

After a respectable time, Rev. Sagal brings in coffee and cookies, and invites us all to his office — turns out it holds way more people than I thought. César, Elenita, and Dolores snuggle next to their parents and grandmother, and Señor and Señora Chávez share their incredible story.

By some miracle, they escaped the raid in Chicago, they tell us. "We got off the train to get food in the station. We thought it was safe, but all of a sudden, border agents were everywhere with their guns," Señor Chávez tells us though their lawyer, Ms. Dean. "When we saw what was happening, we hid in a closet full of brooms and buckets until la Migra was gone."

Señora Chávez picks up the story. "By the time we could safely leave the closet, our children were gone and we did not know what had happened to them. Maybe la Migra snatched them? Maybe they were still on the train? We did not know." The memory is still raw.

Señor and Señora Chávez did the only thing they could. They hopped the next train going toward Ohio and hoped that somehow their children had made it safely to their grandmother. Days later, they learned the dreaded news. Dolores, Elenita, and César were not in Melard.

"It was very dangerous for my mother and her compañero, José, to hide us at their house," Señora Chávez says, "but they welcomed us." She smiles her gratitude toward her mother and José, who has slipped through the door to stand next to Abuela. "Together we tried to figure out what to do to find our children."

Señor Chávez looks at us. His eyes glisten. "Nuestra familia ha sufrido muchas cosas, pero perder a nuestros hijos fue el mayor dolor de todos. No soportamos el dolor."

"Our family has suffered many things, but losing our children was the greatest sorrow of all. It was almost too much to bear," Ms. Dean translates softly.

"We asked Ms. Dean to help us." Señor Chávez pauses. "And then we had a miracle—two miracles. First, we got a package. It went to the wrong person first, but finally got to us." She means the drawings, the Polaroid shot and Dolores's note. "We were so happy. Our hearts soared."

"And the very next morning," Señora Chávez says, "another miracle! Ms. Dean comes with the newspaper. It's Mr. Johnson's story."

"You know the rest," Señor Chávez says. "Here we are with our children in our arms. Thank you—all of you." Both Señor and Señora Chávez tear up again. "By God's grace our family is together again."

When Ms. Dean finishes her translation, Señor and Señora Chávez repeat the last sentence in Spanish, "Por la gracia del Señor, nuestra familia está junta de nuevo," and they make the cross sign over their hearts. It's a silent prayer. Even I know that, and I'm not even Catholic.

The day ends with a lot of tearful good-byes. Dolores is right, it is both a sad and a happy day. And it is a day filled with trepidation. Dolores, Elenita, and César have left us to go hide in the shadows again. They are with their family, but the dangers of discovery, detention, and deportation remain. They are never safe. And the worst fear hangs on them still: Their family can get split apart again. At any moment, agents may bang on their door in the middle of the night and take them all away.

EPILOGUE

The *Central Ohio Star*
Sunday Edition—September 5, 1954
Operation Wetback Uproots a Million Lives
Tears Families Apart
Thomas R. Johnson
Analysis

President Eisenhower's Operation Wetback anti-immigrant campaign has come to our state, and the migrant families from Mexico who travel north to harvest Ohio crops now live in constant fear of detention, deportation, and family separation. This reporter has seen the human face of this ill-advised policy through the eyes and the painful story of one Mexican immigrant family.

Operation Wetback launched this spring when hundreds of Border Patrol agents descended on towns in

California and Texas. The Patrol initiated a full-scale military-style roundup of migrant workers who have crossed the border from Mexico, and over the summer, the federal government has expanded the mass deportation campaign. Border agents have made their way into middle America including cities like Chicago, where large numbers of Mexican immigrants work in factories and on surrounding farms. The agents, wielding guns and badges, show up unannounced in cotton fields, citrus farms, and cattle ranches. They swoop down on Mexican and Mexican-American communities where immigrant families live. The agents fan out through train and bus stations, parks, hotels, and restaurants searching for undocumented Mexican workers. The goal is simple: to round up and deport as many Mexicans as possible, as quickly as possible with little to no regard for constitutional protections against unlawful arrest.

The Mexican migrant-worker family I have come to know — I will call them the Castro family to hide their identity — fled the Border Patrol's Operation Wetback raids in Texas and made their way toward Ohio. The father, mother, and three children risked their lives to hop freight trains hobo-style and come north to reunite with a grandmother who lives in a small agricultural community not far from Columbus. They believed they could find safety in Ohio.

Every spring for years, the family of five has crossed the border into the United States to harvest agricultural crops in Texas and California. When the harvest season is done, they have always returned home to Mexico. But this year was different. Instead of picking strawberries and oranges as they had been hired to do, Operation Wetback raids forced them to flee the fields and hide in a boxcar they hoped was headed to Ohio.

They traveled for days with little water and even less food. When the train reached Chicago, the family was desperate for supplies, so the parents risked coming out of hiding to purchase what they needed. The three children remained hidden in the train car under the care of the oldest daughter.

Operation Wetback is the brainchild of Harlan Carter, head of the Border Patrol, and Joseph Swing, appointed by President Eisenhower to head the federal government's Immigration and Naturalization Service (INS). The term "wetback" is a racial slur against Mexican migrants wading across the Rio Grande to enter the United States. The Border Patrol has boasted that agents nab 2,000 undocumented immigrants a day. At that rate, the total number of detained and deported Mexican migrant workers could total more than one million by the end of the year.

The Castros' desperate decision to buy food in Chicago quickly turned bad. While they were buying their supplies, the Border Patrol staged a surprise raid at Chicago's Union Station. Mr. and Mrs. Castro avoided arrest by hiding in a janitor's closet, but by the time the raid was over, the train carrying their children was gone. The three minors, ranging in age from five to thirteen, were forced to continue the boxcar trip alone without knowing the fate of their parents.

"It was like our mother and father disappeared into the air," the oldest of the Castro children says. "We were afraid we would never see them again." Likewise, the parents had no information about their children, and worried they had been scooped up in the Chicago raid and taken to a detention center. Losing their children was the Castros' greatest fear. Families separated by the Border Patrol may never find each other again.

But this story ends well — sort of. The courage and perseverance of both the Castros and many good people along the way have won out. The Castro family was reunited this past weekend, but the joy of the moment is clouded by the reality that the family has moved back into the shadows again. They must hide. And wait. And hope that our leaders in Washington, DC, will finally enact an immigration policy that respects the rights and dignity of all involved.

ACKNOWLEDGMENTS

I am profoundly grateful for the many who helped make *In the Shadows* a reality. My daughter, Heather Dean, deserves special thanks for comments on the manuscript and especially for her detailed edits and suggestions for the multiple Spanish-language sections.

ABOUT THE AUTHOR

Carol Richardson spent nearly twenty-five years in Washington, DC, as an activist promoting equitable and humane U.S. policies in Latin America. As part of that work, she traveled frequently to Mexico, Central and South America, and across the United States. She recently participated in the 75-mile *Migrant Trail Walk for Life* in the Sonora Desert to help raise alarms and awareness about U.S. immigration policies.

Carol has four teenage grandchildren, and she volunteers for a middle school reading program. She hopes to encourage another generation of engaged, active citizens. Before moving to Washington, DC, Carol was an ordained pastor in the United Methodist Church. Now retired, she lives in Ohio. This is her second book for middle school readers. You can find her first book, *Eight Acres and a Cow*, on Amazon and all major online retailers.

www.ingramcontent.com/pod-product-compliance
Lightning Source LLC
Chambersburg PA
CBHW031949240626
47153CB00003B/914